CW01429488

AUTHOR PHOTOGRAPH BY KATHRIN SIMON

LINDA OLSSON WAS BORN in Stockholm, Sweden, in 1948. She graduated from the University of Stockholm with a law degree, and worked in law and finance until she left Sweden in 1986. What was intended as a three-year posting to Kenya then became a meandering tour of the world with stops in Singapore, the UK and Japan, until she settled in New Zealand with her family. Linda's first novel *Let Me Sing You Gentle Songs* was published in New Zealand in 2005 and became an international success, selling hundreds of thousands of copies in Scandinavia, Europe, the United States, Japan, Korea and in two Chinese versions. It was followed by *Sonata for Miriam* in 2008 and *The Kindness of Your Nature* in 2011.

Also by Linda Olsson

Let Me Sing You Gentle Songs (2005)
Sonata for Miriam (2008)
The Kindness of Your Nature (2011)

LINDA OLSSON

THE BLACKBIRD SINGS AT DUSK

PENGUIN BOOKS

PENGUIN

UK | USA | Canada | Ireland | Australia
India | New Zealand | South Africa | China

Penguin is an imprint of the Penguin Random House
group of companies, whose addresses can be found
at global.penguinrandomhouse.com.

Penguin
Random House
New Zealand

First published in English by
Penguin Random House New Zealand, 2016

1 3 5 7 9 10 8 6 4 2

Text © Linda Olsson, 2016

The moral right of the author has been asserted.

All rights reserved. Without limiting the rights under
copyright reserved above, no part of this publication may
be reproduced, stored in or introduced into a retrieval
system, or transmitted, in any form or by any means
(electronic, mechanical, photocopying, recording or
otherwise), without the prior written permission of both
the copyright owner and the above publisher of this book.

Cover illustration by Imperiet.dk

Text design by Carla Sy © Penguin Random House
New Zealand

Author photograph by Kathrin Simon

Printed and bound in Australia by Griffin Press,
an Accredited ISO AS/NZS 14001 Environmental
Management Systems Printer

A catalogue record for this book is available from the
National Library of New Zealand.

ISBN 978-0-14-357366-1
eISBN 978-1-74-348711-2

penguinrandomhouse.co.nz

MIX
Paper from
responsible sources
FSC
www.fsc.org   FSC® C009448

For Thomas, who never doubted

V

I do not know which to prefer,
The beauty of inflections
Or the beauty of innuendoes,
The blackbird whistling
Or just after.

— From 'Thirteen Ways of Looking at
a Blackbird' by Wallace Stevens

Prologue

THE WIND HAD LIFTED from the Quay at Stadsgården, and gained momentum as it struck the steep cliff-side on its way south. It carried its own dry, paralysing chill, but it had also absorbed some of the dampness and icy coldness of the black water down in the harbour where the ice had just broken. Once up at Mosebacke, the wind took a run and charged mercilessly on through the narrow streets.

Abruptly, the bells of the Katarina Church struck two. The sound was sharp and shrill. There was nothing out there to receive it and soften it. It fell from the bells and gushed out over the churchyard with its dry, dead lawns where the bare trees stood stiff and black, unable to offer any resistance.

1

THE DOORBELL HAD SOUNDED a couple of times. Eventually, she had rolled up a piece of toilet paper and wedged it inside. Since then, she'd not heard it. Whether because nobody had pressed the button, or because the wad of paper was doing its job, she didn't know. Without this intervention she would have had either to put up with the ringing until whoever was at the door gave up, or ask them to leave her alone. She didn't think she could do that. She didn't trust her voice any more, didn't know whether it would still carry. With every day, she became more uncertain.

The apartment had become a shell that enveloped her. It was not a part of her, but her protection. Most of her belongings were still in boxes. Belongings. What an odd word. It certainly did not describe the relationship she had with these things. They no longer belonged to her. She hadn't even bothered checking what she was packing; it had all happened in such a rush. She had no need for any of these things and could not see that she would ever unpack the boxes.

Sounds seeped in from various sources. From the stairwell,

from the street, from neighbouring apartments. A chair scraped across the floor above. Footsteps. And, most difficult of all, distant voices. Small sounds, signs of life, like sharp claws on her skin.

Then the church bells. The constantly recurring sound of the church bells, meaningless measures of time. It was March. She had been here almost two months. And it was Monday, she thought. Or perhaps Tuesday?

She still had some soup left. A few packets of sachets. But the fridge and the pantry were beginning to look bare. It was a little worrying. She wasn't sure what she would do when she ran out completely. Go without until her body gave up? How long would that take? And if that was the ultimate goal, why not speed up the process and throw out the remaining food? She pushed the thought aside. Heaved it in among the others and banged the door closed. Tried to make herself empty again. No thoughts. With her eyes closed she wished for a state of nothingness. Was this too much to ask?

When she lay still, patiently — and her patience had reached unprecedented heights — the Woman in Green would sometimes appear. Just as she used to in her feverish dreams as a child. Always so still by her piano, turned away with her narrow back facing the audience. And never a sound. Never a movement. Just that ominous, pregnant stillness, bringing with it a sickening hopelessness, never articulated yet overwhelming. A nausea that clung to her skin and her tongue. And completely outside her control.

When they had started again she thought they were the same, these visions or whatever they were. She would lie there, drifting in and out of sleep, her forehead clammy and her body burning hot, as if she were running a fever. Then she would be overcome by the nausea, and the dumb and immobile presence would appear, utterly lifelike. On the surface so very peaceful, yet inducing such intense feelings of fear and despair.

She could not remember when she had first met the Woman in Green. It seemed she had always existed, in the darkness beyond reality. When she was a child the dread was such that even the slightest inkling of a bout of fever would completely paralyse her. Not that the vision was frightening in itself; in fact quite the opposite. Nothing ever happened. The Woman in Green never did anything, said anything. She remained still, turned away, locked inside her gloomy world.

As the years went by, the visions stopped, and Elisabeth thought she had outgrown them, but now they were back, and she was as helpless as she had been as a child. There was no protection, no escape. But curiously, the visits — as she had started to refer to them — were also alluring. She had slowly started to long for them. They were as forbidding as ever — perhaps even more so — but they had undergone a subtle transformation. It was hard to put your finger on the difference. If she were to try to put it into words, she would say that a sense of contact had been established. A kind of communication-less communication. It was as though they were both waiting for something to begin.

So now she lay down with a sense of heavy anticipation. She let the darkness embrace her. And she waited.

But suddenly a sound destroyed the stillness she had so carefully created, and in an instant dissolved the sense of anticipation that had filled her. The muted doorbell clicked several times. Her attempt at silencing it had only served to create a far more insidious noise.

Silence again.

She lay still, thinking of someone standing outside her door.

Eventually there was a knock on the door. Once. Then once more, more insistent. She felt herself clench her teeth and close her fists, as if preparing for an attack. Which it was, this encroachment. She sat up in bed, resting on her elbows. She listened. Held her breath and waited.

A scraping sound. A voice.

'Hello! Anybody there?' It sounded like a young man.

A pause.

'I have a parcel for you. It got delivered to me by mistake.'

Clearly he was expecting a response.

She held her breath.

'I'll leave it here by the door if that's okay. It doesn't fit the letter slot.'

She waited.

The sound of the metal flap closing.

Had he peeped inside? Seen her darkness? If so, surely he would have assumed there was nobody home?

At last, real silence and stillness again. She sank back onto the pillow, realising her face was damp with cold sweat.

Abruptly, like a slap in the face, the sound of the letter flap being opened again.

'Well, bye then.'

As if he knew she was hiding inside.

She heard the faint sound of steps across the landing, and a door closing.

She exhaled, closed her eyes for a moment, then got up and walked to the kitchen.

———

WITHOUT TURNING ON THE light, she groped for the glass she knew was on the bench and filled it with water from the tap. She drank slowly, trying to work out what time it might be. Not that it mattered. It felt as though time was a language spoken out there, in another world — a language that she, when her existence had a brush with reality, was forced to try to interpret.

What she really wanted to know was whether she could safely open her front door and pick up the parcel without risking being seen. She didn't want to leave it there to attract the curiosity of neighbours and cause them to try to make contact. She stood by the window, looking out. It was dark, but no longer winter dark. The sky seemed like a slightly transparent skin stretched over something a touch lighter behind.

The street was deserted, so she assumed it must be late. She walked to the front door and paused for a moment with her hand on the door handle before she cautiously opened the door a chink. The stairwell lay in darkness. She quickly bent down and picked up the parcel. It was not really a parcel, more like a padded envelope. But he had been right: it was too thick to fit through the letter slot.

She took a few deep breaths. She did not want this contact. She did not want to be reminded of the world outside. It was bad enough with the mail that arrived on the doormat. She had collected it in a pile on the kitchen table and tried not to think about it. As she added this packet to the top of the pile, she suddenly wondered why she had not just thrown the mail in the rubbish as it arrived. Why had she collected these unwelcome signs of life? She'd never look at them.

But this envelope was different somehow. In an instant this item had created an obligation towards the person who had placed it outside her door. It had established a relationship between them, this invisible neighbour and herself. She had no wish for a relationship of any kind, with anybody, and it pained her to feel this enforced sense of gratitude.

She paced back and forth between the kitchen and the living room in annoyance. Picking up the envelope again, she flicked it against her palm. She could simply throw it away. But that wouldn't change anything. Her neighbour had done her a favour, however unwelcome. She dropped it on the kitchen table and returned to the living room. There, she pulled open the flaps of one of her many boxes of books. She ran her hands over the top layer and picked up a couple. Strangely, her hands remembered what she had suppressed. The moment she held a book in her hands, she knew which one it was. And thereby also which box this was. It was not the one she was after so she opened two more. There it was. She took out the slim volume and stood up. Before she had time to change her mind, she stepped out into the unlit stairwell and tiptoed across the cold marble floor to the neighbour's door.

The brass plate on the door said 'E. Blom'. So, the mistake was understandable. On her own door it said just 'Blom'. Maybe the pile on her kitchen table contained mail intended for this E. Blom? It had never occurred to her to check whether the letters were actually addressed to her.

She propped the book against the wall beside his door. She was not sure why she'd chosen that particular book. All she had to go on was his young voice. And the fact that he had sensed that she was inside. She knew he had. And that he had taken the trouble to say goodbye. Somehow, she couldn't stop thinking about it.

Letters to a Young Poet. Rainer Maria Rilke. Tattered and dog-eared. And probably completely wrong, but there it was anyway. No thank you note. He might not understand what it was for, or from whom. It didn't matter. As far as she was concerned, she was relieved of the obligation. The debt had been paid and they were even.

The silence and peace slowly returned. She sat down at the kitchen table. The package itself was of no interest whatsoever: she added it to the pile. There was only one more thing to do and she could return to her darkness.

She turned on the small lamp on the windowsill and opened the black diary on the table. Picked up the pen and began to write. She didn't really know why she did it. Or for whom. It used to make her existence clearer. Illuminate the incomprehensible. But for some reason it had come to feel completely meaningless. Like a ritual without a purpose. There was nothing left to understand. Yet she kept it up. Short notes, once or twice a day.

Once she had finished, it took her a long time to recapture her darkness.

2

HE FOUND THE BOOK the following afternoon. He'd worked the better part of the night and slept till well into the day. He was on his way out when he spotted it. It was obvious it had not landed there by accident. Fallen from someone's briefcase or pocket. No, it was propped there neatly and deliberately. No card or message of any kind, but he knew who had left it there.

He'd noticed her on the day she moved in. A dark figure hurriedly crossing the street where slushy snow was ankle deep, leading the way for the removal men. Although this was the only time he had seen her, he was sure she was the person living there. He couldn't explain why; he just knew. He'd felt like an idiot crouching down shouting through the letter slot, with his stupid 'Well, bye then,' but he didn't regret it. Obviously she wanted to be left alone: even he got that. But there could be something the matter. Perhaps she was dead? No, she wasn't. Of that he was somehow sure. He knew she'd been in there, behind the closed door, and had heard him. And now the book by his door was confirmation.

A book. She had given him a book. She could have no idea what a stupid choice that was. How hard it was for him to get through even the shortest text. Still, he'd picked it up, turned it over in his hands, started to plod through the blurb on the back cover. *Letters to a Young Poet.* Worse and worse. It couldn't have been more wrong. He threw the book aside.

But when he got back home that evening he picked it up again. As usual, when trying to read, he took out his drawing pad and his pencils, brushes and ink. Other people read for pleasure: he had never understood that. For him it was hard labour. So painful that he tried to avoid it. The entire process was associated with things he had tried to put behind him. Memories from school. The very word: dyslexic. Mother. All the shit that he tried to keep outside the door.

Interpreting the letters and making them into words caused terrible stress. The sharp black signs on the page pushed themselves into his head, but without context or order. And then they danced in there, mockingly inaccessible.

Even though there were books on his shelves, they were relics of the past. If he managed to labour through them once, he never opened them again. Instead, the words were absorbed into the piles of paper and pads that filled shelf after shelf of his living room and hall. In those drawing pads all the texts were turned into a form he could interpret. Every word, every sentence he had managed to decipher was inside the pictures he created.

When he first got to know him, Otto had given him books, too. Otto had picked book after book from his overloaded shelves and handed them to Elias. 'You just have to read this one,' and 'Are you telling me you haven't read this?' It was some time before he was able to tell Otto that he would never get through most of them. Thick classics of five or six hundred pages. Tiny print on yellowed paper. That was when Otto began to tell him the books instead. He didn't read them, just told them from memory. He clearly thought he was being considerate, and that it would not remind Elias of his disability if they were stories, not texts. And he was right, it did feel better. For both of them. Elias couldn't tell how well Otto's versions matched the originals, but he didn't care.

So here he was now, struggling through the slim book one word at a time. It was windy outside the window and the glass made light cracking sounds, but Elias paid no attention. He was completely absorbed. In the circle of light from the desk lamp he drew picture after picture. He had pushed aside his almost-finished project. It would have to wait.

It took him a week.

By then he had filled almost the entire pad. And learnt Rilke's *Letters to a Young Poet* more or less by heart.

When he finished the book he did one more, separate drawing. Now, as he held it up in front of him, he could recite the text more or less word for word:

> *This above all — ask yourself in the stillness of your night: must I write? Delve into yourself for a deep answer. And if this should be affirmative, if you may meet this earnest question with a strong and simple 'I must,' then build your life according to this necessity; your life even into its most indifferent and slightest hour must be a sign of this urge and a testimony to it.*

He looked at the image and realised he had exchanged the word 'draw' for 'write'. And to this question he had a clear answer.

At the bottom of the sheet he wrote:

'Yes, I must.'

He folded the drawing in half and stuck it into the book adjacent to the relevant portion of text.

It was late. Or early, depending on how you looked at it. He pulled on his jacket and boots and picked up the book. He walked across the landing and stood for a moment outside her door. All was still and silent. He bent down and propped the book just as he had found it, but this time against her door frame.

Outside, it was completely dark. He huddled in the deep alcove outside the front door of the building, zipping his jacket up tight, pulling on his knitted hat and gloves. He looked up at the dark sky. His breath was like white smoke in the cold air, quickly dissolving above his head.

Dawn was still hours away. This was his time. He walked briskly across the churchyard and turned right towards Mosebacke. He met nobody.

3

SHE STOOD IN THE unlit kitchen and had just brought the glass of water to her lips when she heard footsteps out in the stairwell. It was too late for a returning neighbour, and too early for the newspaper delivery man. Besides, she had not heard the front door open. The footsteps stopped outside her door, then all was silent. She tiptoed into the hallway. Was he standing there outside her door in the middle of the night? It was an unpleasant thought. Frightening, even. She held her breath and listened attentively.

She heard a faint sound. She couldn't quite tell what it was — not a rustling and not a thud. Just an insignificant little sound that somehow seemed to indicate that the person on the other side of the door was up to something. Was he going to open the letter slot again? Instinctively, she took a couple of steps back and stood alert. But there was no sound from the muted doorbell and no rattling of the letter flap. Nothing at all. What normal person would ring the doorbell of a neighbour he didn't know in the middle of the night anyway? Unless there was an emergency. But the cautious, slow steps certainly didn't indicate any urgency. She kept listening.

The sound of steps again, across the landing and down the short staircase. The sound of the front door opening and closing.

She walked quickly to the bedroom, still holding the glass of water, and peeked down at the street.

It was a moment before she saw him: he must have stopped in the doorway for a bit. But there he was. Tall, and loping along with long rapid strides. Leather jacket and a knitted hat. She would have been hard pressed to give any further description. Yet there was already something familiar about him. She shook her head. What a stupid thought. But here was a figure to add to the voice she had heard earlier. E. Blom. What did the E stand for? Erik? That was the only man's name she could think of that matched his age. Nobody was called Evald, Einar or Evert any more. Or were they? It was a long time since she had had a reason to think about Swedish men's names. Any name, for that matter.

She put the glass down on the bench and returned to the front door. All was quiet again as she cautiously inched the door open. The stairwell lay in semi-darkness, lit only by the outside light over the front door to the building. But she saw it immediately. The book. There it was, propped just as she had left it by the door across the landing. She snorted with irritation. Had he rejected her gesture of gratitude? After sitting on it for over a week? She had been convinced that the balance had been restored. That she owed him nothing.

She picked it up and a folded sheet of paper fell to the floor. Catching it in mid-air she stepped back inside, closing the door quietly behind her.

She sat down at the kitchen table. Hesitated, then reached out and switched on the lamp on the windowsill. In spite of herself she gave a start at the sudden shock of light, and squeezed her eyes shut for a moment. When she opened them again, her gaze landed on the pile of unopened mail. She pushed it to one side and placed the book and the paper on the table in front of her. She slowly unfolded the sheet of paper.

She had no idea what to expect. Some kind of note, perhaps. An explanation as to why he had returned the book. A thank you, even. But it was neither. It was a drawing — a black and white ink drawing. She didn't recognise the image; the shapes were figurative and they intertwined to form a kind of uniform whole. A pattern of sorts, in which every detail was exquisitely controlled and unique.

She couldn't for the life of her make out what it was supposed to be, if anything at all. Something was written along the bottom edge of the paper. 'Yes, I must.' Just that. She snorted again and dropped the paper on the table. What did that mean? It made no sense. Was it some kind of bookmark? Something not meant for her?

She pulled the book towards her and it fell open at a page that had obviously been read recently. She bent forward and started to read. At a glance she recognised the passage: she had read it many times before. Had transcribed it into her notebook when she was still at school.

This above all — ask yourself in the stillness of your night . . .

He had not just read the book, but absorbed its content. And he obviously wanted to let her know that he had. He was saying thank you.

She stood up. She struggled to breathe as she refilled the glass from the tap and drank slowly.

Stupid, she thought. Ridiculous and pathetic. Why did I bring the damned thing inside?

She closed her eyes and took another mouthful of water.

So now I am in debt to him again! Damned drawing! Damned book! She grabbed them both and threw them across the kitchen.

But there was no way she could hold back the tears.

4

HE WORKED BEST EVENINGS and nights, but since he had started the new project, increasingly often he woke early and sat down at his drawing table straight away. It was a long time since he had felt like this. The story and the images flowed so naturally. He seemed to recall it had been like this with his very first book, but back then he had no idea what he was doing. It had just been a matter of survival: drawing in order to cling to life a little longer. Trying not to think too far ahead.

The thought of it becoming a book had never entered his mind. But it did become a book, and then there was another one. And eventually a job. What Mother had called 'Elias's hobby' and Gunnar had called his 'fucking scrawling' had actually turned into a job that paid rent and food. And a bit besides.

He'd given the new folder on the computer a title. *The Blackbird.* Not that she sang, exactly. In fact he'd never heard her utter a sound. Hardly seen her, for that matter. Just caught a glimpse of a dark figure in a heavy coat and winter hat. The pictures he was drawing had nothing to do with who she might actually be.

They were just his fantasies about an invisible neighbour. Here he was, day in and day out making up a story about a woman he had never met.

He had made her into a bird, which was completely perverse if you thought about it. But he was not going to think about it for a second. He wanted to stay in this mood. Maintain this excitement. Because that was how it felt: his job had become exciting again. When he picked up his pencil and began to sketch he had no idea what would emerge. Yet he didn't feel the slightest hesitation and once completed, every drawing was perfectly formed.

He had no idea what to do about the text. He had assumed that Maja would write it for him, as she always did, and it was a huge blow when she declined. Her own novel had finally been accepted for publication and polishing that took all her time now. All he could do was to congratulate her and be pleased for her.

So he had to find someone else, but he had no idea where to start. Maja could read him so well. Often she just had to see a drawing once and she'd come up with the right words, as if she thought exactly as he did. She knew him inside out and they'd been making up stories together since they met on the first day of school. She had the words; he had the pictures. It was not a question of one leading the other: they were equally essential.

There was nothing he could do about it now. If this were to become a book, someone else would have to write the words eventually, but for now the pictures were enough. He wasn't going to dwell on the future.

When he heard Otto banging on the floor upstairs he looked up, a little surprised. The whole day had gone and it was time for dinner. Reluctantly, Elias put down his pen and stood up, his eyes still on the unfinished drawing. Inside his head, he could see the whole story play out. He felt a surge of frustration. He had the story, but there was no way he could write it down. It was like hearing music inside your head, beautiful music, but not being able to sing or play a note. Locked inside his head, the story was worthless. It didn't really exist.

He tore himself away from his desk and went to the bathroom, where he undressed. He stood under the shower, closed his eyes and let the water pour over his face. In a way, it was fitting, the fact that he had only half the skills required. He was half in every way. His whole fucking life was a half-life. He could sit here and draw his fucking pictures and listen to his own stories. But what kind of life was that, if you stopped to think about it?

He turned off the water, dried himself and dressed again.

He went upstairs to Otto's.

5

EVERY TIME OTTO REMINDED himself that he had lived in this apartment longer than anywhere else it surprised him. Fifteen years this May.

He had stayed on in the townhouse in Västertorp for three years after Eva died. Thinking back, he was intrigued by the fact that he had not packed up and left earlier. He'd never really felt comfortable there. Never regarded it as his home. It had been like a kind of structure to house Eva. Inside, she had created her own world and he had always felt like a piece of furniture that was tolerated but didn't quite fit in.

There was something in Eva's past that she was trying to hold back. Something she never talked about. Yet Otto had intuitively understood how hard she worked at keeping the past at bay. She wanted to remove herself from it physically, escape as far from it as possible, and this ugly little house seemed to give her a sense of security. He, too, had sometimes felt as if it were at the end of the world. The last house in a row of identical townhouses bordering a small piece of woodland. Sometimes he thought the house was leaning away from the others, trying to break loose and venture into the wood.

The house itself *was* ugly. He'd thought so the first time he saw it, and he hadn't changed his mind during the years they had lived there. A square beige box, joined on one side to its identical square beige twin. There was not much of a garden either, just a small patch at the back, shaded by a large fir that dropped its acidic needles over the struggling lawn. This did have its advantages: he never had to mow the lawn. The grass seemed to just stay alive but it never grew. Neither he nor Eva had taken any interest in the garden. Sometimes he'd wondered if the neighbours would have liked them to make an effort. Plant tulips and crocus, prune the hedge. Generally behave the way other neighbours did.

They never socialised with the neighbours; just exchanged greetings over the sparse hedge. During the first few years the neighbours had been a couple of similar age to themselves. They'd had a bit more conversation with them but it had never developed into friendship. Eva had not wanted that. What he might have wanted was never considered.

Then a younger family with children moved in, and the contact became even more sporadic. Otto had not exactly missed having a social life, not then. But these days he wondered whether a different kind of life might have been an option.

After Eva died he knew the house was too big for one person. But it was economical and he had no strong incentive to do anything about his situation, so time went by.

When he thought about it he realised that it was only as a small child that he'd had the feeling of living in a proper home. Those first few years before they moved to Sweden. They had lived in a one-bedroom apartment, all four of them. When his little sister Elsa was still alive. The apartment was on the second floor of a solid, four-storey stone building. In the winter there was always snow. (He knew that could not be right, but that was how he chose to remember it. Always snow, all winter. Masses of it to wade through and to play in. Snow that muted all sound.) Inside, it was always warm and cosy. They had a small coal stove in the kitchen that seemed to warm the entire place. Upstairs lived the Schmidt family, and downstairs were the Berlingers, with Miss Blumenthal on the other side of the wall. It was as if they, too, helped keep his family warm just by their presence, like some form of human insulation.

In Stockholm, although again they lived in an inner-city apartment, it was not the same. Nothing had ever been the same. But it wouldn't have been, of course, even if they had stayed in Vienna. Everything changes. It's only what we have lost that seems immutable.

In the beige townhouse in Västertorp he'd often felt cold — colder inside than out. When he finally sold up and bought this apartment, it was not a considered decision. He didn't move *to* something; he fled *from* something. One day he just knew he had to get out of that house. He didn't think of his new place as permanent — not then, not now. Actually, he didn't think much about it at all. For the first time in his life he'd made his own decision about where to live, how to live, even though he was not convinced he was equal to the task. He just couldn't face staying on in the house any longer. Where he went didn't seem to matter.

The furniture was still where it had happened to land the day he moved in. It was like a hotel room, or a storage space for his belongings — and his person. Somewhere to sleep until a more permanent solution presented itself. And he'd lived like this for over fifteen years. The temporary had somehow made itself permanent.

He stood by the stove stirring the casserole while looking about the small space that was his kitchen.

I haven't bought any of this, he reflected. They are Eva's chairs, her table. Even the pot on the stove she chose. And the spoon I'm holding. The only thing I can truly claim as mine is the lamp.

The original light fitting he had brought with him had broken a few years after he moved in. He bought a replacement from a small antique shop near Odenplan. Not that he'd been in search of a lamp that day. He just happened to walk past the shop during his lunch break and saw it in the window — a small antique glass chandelier. It was completely misplaced where it was hanging now, of course, but he liked it. It spread a warm yellow light over the table yet left the outer edges of the room in a comforting semi-darkness. Every time he turned it on it gave him pleasure to watch the reflections of the small prisms.

He didn't often think of Eva now, at least not consciously. But for many years after her death he'd woken up every morning with his left arm stretched out as if searching for her. Strange, as there had never been any warmth in Eva. She was not a warm person in any sense of the word. It was only after she was gone that he realised he'd never loved her. He'd been in awe of her. Entranced by her beauty. Overwhelmed by the fact that she had wanted him. He used to think of her as an alabaster statuette, perfect in every detail. But cold.

He was brought out of his thoughts by the sound of the front door opening and Elias calling out from the hallway.

'Come in. I'm here in the kitchen,' he replied. 'I've made veal stew with dill. I hope that's okay.'

'Smells great,' Elias said, and sat down on one of the kitchen chairs.

They had first met the day Elias moved in. Otto happened to come home as Elias was carrying his things into his apartment. He'd introduced himself and the young man seemed to appreciate it. He put down the box he was holding and stretched out his hand.

'Hi, I am Elias Blom. I've taken over my grandmother's apartment. She died just before Christmas.'

'Yes, I heard. My condolences. A truly lovely lady.'

There was a moment of silence.

'Well, welcome to our building. I hope you will settle in well. Nice to see some young people here. I live upstairs. My floor is your ceiling. If there's anything you need, just knock on my door.'

There was another silence, but neither man made a move to leave.

'I suppose it'll take you a while to get sorted,' the older man said. 'If you feel like it, you're most welcome to come upstairs once your things are inside. I'll find something to eat, even if it's just a sandwich. If you feel like it. If it suits.'

That first meeting had been the start of a deep friendship. They met at least once a week. Sometimes just over a quick cup of coffee, sometimes to discuss some aspect of Elias's work. Sometimes to 'read' a book together, which involved Elias lying stretched out on the sofa while Otto sat in his armchair and 'told' him one of his books. Eventually they had begun a routine of having dinner together on Tuesday nights. Always at Otto's, and always announced by Otto banging on his living-room floor when it was time for Elias to make his way upstairs.

Otto didn't know much about Elias's private life, and he hadn't talked much about his own background either. They stuck to the present. To art and books and music. That was enough.

The two apartments were identical in layout, though you wouldn't have believed it looking at them. While Elias's space was painted white, sparsely furnished and entirely dedicated to his work, Otto's was an overstuffed storage space for everything he had lugged with him from his previous existence.

Elias preferred Otto's apartment; he didn't consider his own a proper home. It was just a workplace where he also happened to sleep. Otto's place, on the other hand, was filled with personal objects, with music, with smells of delicious food and . . . well, life. Otto, for his part, was in awe of Elias's apartment, which seemed to be twice the size of his own, and always alive with some creative project.

When he had first seen inside Elias's apartment, Otto had been filled with mixed feelings. Some to do with himself, some to do with his young neighbour. Otto had never seen anything like it — or at least any apartment like it. It looked nothing like a home. The living space that this young man had created for himself was so barren and so impersonal. There was no room for anything other than work — the whole place was a work space. At first it had unnerved him, but as he got to know Elias he realised how perfectly it suited him. Now it was something close to jealousy that filled him when he popped down to visit. Otto had moved straight from the parental home to living with Eva. He had never had a space that was truly his, created exclusively for him, to suit his needs and to his taste. Seeing the way Elias lived made him wonder what his own home could have looked like.

'Let's eat,' Otto said, and placed the steaming pot on the table.

6

THE TUESDAY DINNERS TOOK a variety of forms. Sometimes it was just a matter of a quick meal and nothing more. Other times they would remain at the kitchen table for hours. Especially if Otto started to talk. But this evening it was Elias who put down his cutlery first. He looked at Otto.

'I've started a new project. I have no idea where it's going, or whether it will turn into anything I can use, but I'm really enjoying it. I haven't felt like this about a project for ages. I'm even getting up in the mornings before nine!'

He looked up and they both smiled.

'It must be special,' said Otto.

'I have no idea. I'll keep going as long as it feels good . . . we'll see. Except that Maja can't help me with the text this time. Not that I know if it will come to that. But her novel has been accepted and she is snowed under with rewriting and editing. Great for her, of course. But if — and it's a big if — this turns into a story I want to publish, I'll need to find another writer.'

They ate in silence for a while.

'So, what is it?'

Elias looked up and hesitated before he answered.

'Well . . . it will sound completely crazy.'

'Try me. I've heard almost everything — or at least read about it.'

'You know the woman who lives in the apartment opposite mine? Her surname is Blom, too. A couple of weeks ago I got a parcel that was meant for her, so I wandered over to give it to her. I rang the bell because it was too thick to fit through the door slot. Then I knocked on the door several times, but nothing. I *knew* she was in there. So I opened the letter slot and called out.'

He looked up with an embarrassed shrug.

'I have no idea why I did it — as I am telling you I can hear how weird it sounds. But that's what I did.'

Otto said nothing, but indicated for Elias to continue.

'Well, I waited for quite a while, but still no sign of her. In the end I just left the parcel by her door and went back to my apartment.'

'It's odd: she must have lived here for a couple of months by now but I haven't even caught a glimpse of her,' said Otto, sipping his beer.

'Exactly. It's really odd. She never leaves the apartment, it always looks dark and there's never a sound. She's definitely in there, because the next day she left a book outside my door. I am not sure why, but I'm certain it was her.'

'A book? Why on earth?'

'Well, I guess it was some kind of thank you. For giving her the parcel. I've read it, actually.'

He smiled and looked at Otto.

'Yeah, I know. But I did. The whole thing. *Letters to a Young Poet* it's called.'

'Rilke,' Otto said.

'It took me a week. I worked my way through it one word at a time. Now I've translated it into images. My language. I've even learnt one paragraph by heart.'

'Hold on!' Otto leapt from his chair and disappeared into the hallway. A moment later he returned holding a slim book. He sat down again and leafed through the book quickly until he found the page he was after. He started to read the exact paragraph.

When he finished he looked at Elias.

'Am I right?'

'Yes. That's the one. You're amazing. Have you read everything?'

Otto made a dismissive gesture.

'So, when I'd finished the whole book I did a drawing of that particular paragraph and wrote down my response, *Yes, I must*, at the bottom of the page. I folded it and put it inside the book, and left it outside her door. And now it's gone so I assume she has it. She probably thinks I'm mad.'

'Does this have anything to do with your project?'

'Yes,' Elias said slowly. 'Yes, it does. Something happened to me when I read that book. I just couldn't stop thinking about it. Wondering why she'd given me that particular one. Whether it was just a random pick, or if she meant something by it. But she doesn't know me, so how could that be? I couldn't stop thinking about her either. I don't even know her name, just that we have the same surname. And I've only had that quick glimpse of her the day when she moved in. With her hat pulled down and her bulky winter coat, at dusk on a grey winter's day. I have no idea what she looks like. Even whether she is young or old. Or why she lives the way she does — never leaves her apartment, never turns on the lights. I assume she doesn't want any contact with her neighbours, but I don't know why. Maybe that's why I can't stop thinking about her. So I started drawing her. At first it was just a little sketch — for fun. Like doodling, you know? Then it turned into a dark shadow over dirty slushy snow. But now . . .'

Elias fell silent.

'Well, now it's a story. The beginnings of a story, anyway. I call it *The Blackbird*.'

They ate in silence. Then Elias put down his fork again.

'In my drawing she becomes a bird. At first, a poor scruffy little bird that's ended up in the wrong place, in every sense of the word. Half dead. And then . . . I couldn't stop wondering what was going to happen to it. Why it ended up here in the middle of winter. And where it was going.'

He looked up.

'I know you'll think it all sounds crazy.'

His fingers traced invisible patterns on the table.

'I'm not going to tell you more. Not yet, anyway. We'll see how it goes.'

Otto cleared his throat.

'It doesn't sound crazy at all. I may not understand it entirely, but I can see how excited it makes you. Just carry on!' He knocked on the book on the table.

'Here you are having read an entire book without *having* to. Imagine that! I think you just need to keep going with it and see where it leads you.'

'I'll carry on for a bit longer, then I'll show you, and you can help me decide if it's worth finishing.'

'I feel honoured, Elias,' said Otto, laughing a little. '*The Blackbird.*' He savoured the words.

Otto stood and started to clear the table. Elias helped, and Otto produced dessert, a homemade apple cake.

'*Turdus merula.*'

'What?'

'That's the Latin name for the blackbird.'

Elias laughed. 'I thought you were talking about the cake.'

Otto smiled and sat down.

'Amazing that it's the national bird of Sweden. You'd think they would have gone for something more . . . well, more uniquely Swedish. Like . . . well, like the ptarmigan. But they chose the blackbird. To me, the blackbird is too exotic for Sweden, too mysterious for this practical country. But its song is so beautiful. Sad and soothing at the same time.'

They sat for a while longer, before Elias stood up.

'Thank you, Otto. Great dinner, as always. I have to go back to my place and do some more work.'

Otto followed him out into the hallway.

At the door, he put his hand lightly on Elias's shoulder.

'Guess what I long for most at this time of year? The return of the blackbird. When it arrives in the courtyard at the back I always open my window so I can hear its song. Nothing lovelier than to sit at the kitchen table at dusk listening to that song. But it will be a while yet.'

7

SOMETHING HAD SHIFTED.

She tried to understand in what way. And why. It was not the weather, which didn't really affect her. The last few days had been still, no wind at all, but the view from the kitchen remained the same. Grey skies, bare trees. A kind of illustrated stillness. It was not markedly lighter, though spring was approaching. No, darkness came to her as before. And so did the Woman in Green. Yet she, too, had somehow subtly changed. There was an increased sense of urgency to their meetings. And also an element of reproach. They still met in complete silence, but it was different in some way she couldn't put her finger on. Was the woman's back a little straighter, her stance a little stiffer? Had the angle of her head changed ever so slightly? Or had the light around her dimmed a fraction, making the shadows longer? Whatever it was, it made her feel there was an accusation in the air. As if she had done something to earn the disapproval of the woman by the piano.

The day was quickly approaching when she would have to make a decision on the food situation. She needed to stock up with fresh food. Even if she brushed her teeth without turning on the bathroom light she could see the blood-streaked saliva in the basin as she rinsed her mouth. It had been a long time since she had eaten fruit or vegetables. Just those damned mugs of soup. But shopping meant getting dressed. Going outside. Meeting people.

However hard she tried, day by day it was getting more difficult to push the thoughts aside.

A week after she received the book with the strange drawing inside, she found a large envelope on the doormat. No name or address, no stamp, just a plain white envelope. She stood staring at it for a moment before picking it up. She didn't open it — just dropped it on the kitchen table. Then she made a cup of tea and paced up and down, mug in hand.

Why didn't she just dump this envelope on top of the pile of other mail and forget about it? For some reason she couldn't make herself do it. When she stopped in the kitchen doorway she could see the gleaming white envelope on the table. She wanted no unwelcome reminders of life outside. Yet, as if pulled against her will, she approached the table. She put down the mug and picked up the envelope. It was not sealed.

Inside, there was a drawing.

It was nothing like the one she'd found inside the book. She ran her fingertips over the sheet of paper. This drawing was not a pattern. It was an image of a black bird against a white background. The bird was so very delicately painted, just a few brushstrokes, yet so alive it might fly off the paper at any moment. It floated against what looked like slushy snow. This, too, looked so real that she felt the chill in her fingertips. She put the picture down but could not take her eyes off it.

It was not an original, that much she could tell. It was a computer printout. She was no expert but she could see that the artist was very, very good. Who was it? There was no signature, no information of any kind. It must have come from the neighbour again. Was it his own work? And why had he given it to her? She was perplexed. It was not exactly threatening but it felt slightly unpleasant. What did he want with her? What was it called when people followed you around? Stalking, that was it. Could it be something like that? No, that was an absurd thought. He didn't know her. They'd never even seen each other.

They'd sorted everything between them, hadn't they? A neighbourly favour, followed by a thank you. She had restored the balance. She should be able to sink back into the soothing darkness, but here he was disturbing the peace again. Pushing his way in.

She swallowed several times, and to her despair she felt her eyes brimming over. I am not sad, she thought. I am justly annoyed. And angry. Angry, that's what I am. At this intrusion. At not being left alone.

She turned the picture upside down and walked to the bedroom where she threw herself on the bed.

But reality continued to intrude. She couldn't close her ears to the sounds from outside, or her eyes to the light that filtered through the gap in the curtains.

It looked as if the sun had come out.

8

IT WAS MONDAY AND Otto was on his way out to do his shopping. Lately, he had taken to slowing down as he passed her door. He didn't stop, of course; that would have seemed suspicious if she registered the comings and goings outside her door. He just crossed the landing more slowly than he used to. Pricked up his ears. But he never heard a sound, never noticed a stirring. And he certainly never saw her.

He realised, a little embarrassed, that he felt a slight disappointment each time. What was he hoping for? How pathetic: a man of nearly seventy years old lurking outside the door of a woman he'd never even set eyes on.

He walked briskly down the steps to the front door and outside.

The last few days had been sunny, but it was a pale sun that gave no warmth. Yet it seemed to draw people outside. He noticed people sitting on the benches along the walkway through the churchyard. Brave, pale figures with their faces turned towards the sky. He had a sudden vision of drowning people desperately gasping for air. It would be another month, at least, before it would be pleasant to sit on those benches. Today there was a raw chill in the air and the sky was slowly darkening. He hoped he would make it home before the rain, and quickened his steps a little. He turned into Östgötagatan.

Ever since he had befriended Elias, Tuesdays had become the hook on which he hung his little life. The rest of the week he just cruised aimlessly. Had someone asked what filled his days he would have struggled to remember. Unless it were a Tuesday. There were his books, of course, but even they had somehow seemed to lose a little of their allure. If he got his hands on a new book, bought or borrowed with anticipation, he would inevitably realise after a few pages that it was vaguely familiar. A version of something he'd already read. It was the same when he turned on the radio, which he did less and less often. The news no longer felt like news. It was history repeating itself, a tragic *perpetuum mobile*.

He enjoyed his daily walks, though. And the thoughts that were generated as he put one foot in front of the other. Sometimes he had a destination in mind but usually he just started walking, only to find himself up at Fåfängan taking in the view over the Old Town, or at Riddarholmen looking back across Riddarfjärden towards Söder, and with no memory of how he'd got there. Meanwhile, his thoughts had taken their own walk. Sometimes into the past, and sometimes they took off in the most surprising directions.

He found himself thinking about Eva. Perhaps the mysterious neighbour had triggered these thoughts. When Eva appeared in his thoughts it was always as an image, never as a live woman. He owned her only as a series of still pictures. She never moved, never said anything. He had no memories of her perfume, or how her skin felt under his hands. Nothing like that. Just pictures that felt posed. Eva at her desk, cigarette in hand. At the piano. Standing by the car.

He had to consciously work out how long it had been. It was eighteen years since Eva had passed away. An eternity, and also no time at all. He had lived here for fifteen years — walked these same streets, done his shopping, gone to the library. And not much else. Perhaps it had been a mistake to sell the shop and retire before he turned sixty. Not that he had retired, exactly. He had stayed on and helped manage the shop for a few years, until he felt that he was no longer contributing anything. He remembered being apprehensive about selling. But the second-hand bookshop was well established, one of the best in the country, and the offer had been very good. He would have enough to live well, if not a life of luxury. Together with what he got when he sold the townhouse, and the money from Eva's life insurance, he certainly had enough. His needs were modest.

They had never spent much, Eva and he. It was odd, really. Eva looked like a woman made for luxury and extravagance but she was not like that at all. On the other hand, there had been no room for negotiation over whatever she *did* want. A small townhouse in Västertorp and an old Volvo Amazon. The odd short holiday in Paris or Rome. That was what she demanded. And she really did: she demanded what she wanted as her right.

Looking back, Otto realised he had been very lucky with the sale of the shop. He probably would not have survived the rapid changes to the industry. He had sold at the right time. After he left for good he took care to avoid the street where the shop was. But it had closed down now. And these days he moved in smaller circles and seldom got to Vasastan. His present walks stretched to Skanstull and down to Hornstull, to Danvikstull and to the Old Town. Very rarely did he have reason to extend his journey further. There was a bookshop in Götgatan, and the library at Medborgarplatsen. Besides, given how he felt about new books nowadays, he might just as well reread the books he already had.

He found he was standing outside the supermarket. The first drops of rain fell from the dark sky as he stepped through the sliding glass doors. He needed to think about what to buy.

Tomorrow was Tuesday.

9

SHE HEARD THE RAIN beating against the window. Rain was good. She liked the sound of it. She wasn't sure if it was the rain that had woken her but she was wide awake. As the odd car passed outside the window she watched the streaks of light cross the ceiling above her bed. The house was silent. It was her time. But she felt restless so she got out of bed.

She had one arm in her dressing gown when she heard the sound. She stopped and listened. It was outside and she couldn't make out what it was. The window was open a chink and she heard what sounded like a muted moaning sound. At first she thought it might be an animal. A cat, perhaps? They made strange sounds in the spring, didn't they? She pulled the dressing gown tight around her and walked to the window. There was nothing to see: the street was empty. Just as she was about to turn away, she thought she saw — or perhaps rather felt — a movement close to the wall, right underneath her window. It was impossible to see what it was without leaning out the window. Another sound. A scraping, like shoes against the pavement — a shuffling noise. Followed by a human voice, but no words that she was able to interpret. Was it a weak cry for help? She slowly opened the window, put her hands on the windowsill and leaned out to take a look.

He was lying on his side, as if seeking protection from the wall. There was so much blood she would never have recognised his face, even if she had known it. But she recognised the leather jacket.

There was nobody else around as far as she could see.

She pulled the window closed. Stood uncertainly for a moment. Then she hurried to her front door, stuck her feet into her boots and stepped into the hallway. Leaving her door open, she ran down the stairs and pushed open the heavy main door.

He had not moved.

She kneeled by his side and put her hand on his wrist. It was icy cold and wet but she could feel a pulse. There was blood everywhere. A deep cut over his eye. And there seemed to be something wrong with his nose: pale blood bubbled from it with every breath. She realised she was making little ineffectual gestures with her hands, as if she didn't know what to do with them. Equally silly and ineffectual sounds came from her mouth. She heard herself moan.

Her neighbour made a wheezing sound and opened the eye that was not swollen shut. He tried to move but his head fell back against the pavement.

Then he said something. She couldn't quite make it out, and bent over closer.

'Get Otto,' he said. 'Otto Vogel. Upstairs.'

He closed his eye again and she watched fresh blood trickle from his mouth. She found she was shivering — whether from cold or from shock she was not sure. She ought to do something for him before she went for help but she couldn't think what, so she stood up and ran inside. She checked the nameplates inside the front door and saw an 'O. Vogel' on the second floor. She hurried up the stairs. She'd rung the doorbell before she could consider what time of day it might be. Or that she was in her dressing gown. Impatiently, she pressed the button a second time and soon she heard steps approaching. The door opened slightly.

'So sorry, but there has been an accident,' she said. 'Your neighbour — my neighbour — has had an accident.' She heard her voice breaking. 'Blom, his name is Blom,' she added. 'He's lying on the pavement just outside the front door. There's blood everywhere and I don't know what to do . . .' Now she was sobbing.

The door opened wide and she stood face to face with a short, older man struggling to get into a striped dressing gown. He wore nothing other than a pair of white underpants and he was barefoot.

'Elias, is it Elias?' he asked.

Without another word she turned and walked quickly ahead of him down the stairs and out into the street.

He was still lying exactly as she had left him.

Otto rushed to his side and fell to his knees. Elisabeth noted that he was still barefoot.

'Elias!' he called out. 'Elias, can you hear me?' He dabbed at the young man's face with the sleeve of his dressing gown. 'Oh, Elias, what have they done to you?' he wept.

Elias opened his eye again.

'Help me,' he said, the words barely audible.

Otto bent forward and took a closer look at Elias's face.

'You need an ambulance, Elias,' he said, and went to stand up but Elias stretched out his hand and Otto sank to his knees again.

'No ambulance,' Elias whispered.

'You need to get to hospital,' said Otto, holding Elias's hand. 'I'll come with you. But you can't stay here — we'll have to try to get you inside.'

'Help me, please.' Otto looked at Elisabeth. 'Help me support him.'

Together they managed to prop Elias up against the wall. His breathing was wheezy and it was obvious he was in great pain.

They stood on either side of him, looking at each other.

'I think we should try to get him inside,' Otto said. He kneeled down again. 'Do you think you can walk up the first few steps if we hold you, Elias?'

Elias stretched out his hands.

'If you come and stand close to the wall for support, and we stick our arms under his, I think we can get him to his feet,' Otto said. 'Let's give it a try.'

Slowly and gently they managed to lift Elias, and for a moment they all three stood leaning against the wall. Then Otto put one of Elias's arms over his shoulder. Elias moaned. Otto prompted Elisabeth to take the other arm.

'One step at a time, one step at a time,' Otto said, as they slowly moved towards the door. He asked Elisabeth to press the buzzer and as it clicked he pushed the door open with his shoulder. All the time Elias was leaning heavily on both of them and for a moment Elisabeth was afraid she would not be able to hold up.

They made it inside the door.

'Now it's just a few steps, Elias, and we'll put you down. Do you have your keys in your pocket?'

Elias made a feeble attempt at shaking his head.

'They took them,' he said, his words barely understandable.

'Can we put him in your place for now?' Otto asked, looking at Elisabeth. She stared back, speechless.

'Just while I run upstairs and throw something on and call a taxi,' he said. 'We have to get him to hospital.'

'Yes, yes of course,' she said. 'It's just not . . . Yes, yes of course.'

Inside her door Elisabeth groped for the light switch. As the light came on she could see how her place must look to others, but she tried to keep her focus on Elias. They led him into her bedroom and gently lowered him onto the bed. The older man seemed oblivious to the state of her apartment. Elisabeth ran to the bathroom and came back with a towel which she gave to Otto, who was sitting on the edge of the bed.

Elias looked even worse in here.

'There's no doubt about it, Elias. You need to go to hospital,' said Otto, gently wiping blood from Elias's face.

He stood up.

'I won't be a minute,' he said to Elisabeth, tying the belt of the dressing gown more tightly.

'Otto. Otto Vogel,' he said, and stretched out his hand.

'Elisabeth. Elisabeth Blom,' she said and took his hand in hers.

'I'll be right back.' He disappeared out the door.

Elisabeth heard the rapid sound of his bare feet as she slowly sat down on the bed. It was difficult to tell whether Elias was conscious. His breathing was uneven and blood still trickled from his nose.

She bent forward and looked at him. And, to her surprise, found herself gently stroking his wet hair.

10

THE TAXI DRIVER, a tall, heavily built man, had his arm around Elias's back, with Otto on the other side. It was a strangely lopsided group that uncertainly traversed the landing and ventured down the stairs, one step at a time.

She stood by her door for a moment and heard the front door open and close. Otto said something to the driver, the car doors banged shut and the taxi drove away.

She walked slowly back to her bedroom and stood in the doorway. There was blood on the pillow and on the sheets. But that was not what caught her attention. She looked around the room, as though she were seeing it for the first time. Which, in a sense, she was.

There was no furniture other than the bed. A few clothes hung on plastic hangers inside the open wardrobe, but everything else was still in three large cardboard boxes along the wall. Another box served as a bedside table. There were no rugs on the wooden floor but there were curtains, though they were not hers. They had come with the apartment, as had the plain lamp globe in the centre of the ceiling. It spread a hard light over the room.

She pulled off the sheets and the pillowcase and took them to the bathroom. Then she made up the bed with fresh linen and sat down at the foot of the bed, her dressing gown pulled firmly across her chest. She was cold. The dressing gown was damp from the rain and her bare feet looked white. She lifted her hand and ran the palm over her cheek. She had no idea what she looked like. She ran her hand through her hair. It felt lank and tangled. She felt exhausted, physically as well as mentally.

Eventually she got up and turned off the light, got into bed and pulled the duvet over her. There were no sounds, inside or out. She lay on her back with her hands folded across her chest.

'This is too hard,' she whispered to the dark room. 'I can't start all over again. Not now. Not ever.'

And she turned over and wept into the pillow.

———

IT WAS STILL COMPLETELY dark. She was tangled up in her dressing gown and soaked in sweat. The Woman in Green sat by her piano with her face partly turned so that her profile was visible. She was still silent but there was no doubt about her irritation. Her reproach. Yet there was something infinitely satisfying in seeing her again. Being in her company. Everything else fell away and there was just the two of them.

This is where I belong, Elisabeth thought. This is how it must be.

She lay absolutely still. Waited.

———

SHE WOKE UP WITH a dry mouth and still sweaty. It was daytime. The sun had not yet reached her window but she could tell it was a bright, clear day.

She disentangled herself from her dressing gown and let it fall to the floor. In the bathroom she stood in front of the mirror. It was dark in the windowless space. She held her hand on the light switch for a moment before flicking it on. The row of small lights above the mirror fluttered a couple of times before steadying, gloomily lighting up her face.

She stared back at the image. Frowned and bent forward. She felt no connection whatsoever with the person she saw. It was as if her memory of herself had been completely erased, and she was not sure she wanted to renew the relationship.

She stepped into the bathtub and turned on the shower. Lathered herself from top to toe. Rinsed. Did it all a second time. And then once more.

When she returned to the bedroom she dug around in the removal boxes until she found a t-shirt and a pair of trackpants.

Just as she was finished, the doorbell rang. Well, it didn't exactly ring. There was just the clicking sound from the muted bell. She stiffened.

Three times, and it stopped.

Three more knocks on the door.

She walked into the hallway, soundlessly on her bare feet.

She heard footsteps just outside the door, which crossed the landing and started up the stairs to the next floor. Very slowly she opened the door and peered through the narrow gap.

'Oh, I'm sorry, it's only me,' Otto said, stepping back down onto the landing. 'I thought you might want to hear how it went.' He crossed to her door. 'At the hospital.'

She didn't respond, but neither did she close the door.

'Four broken ribs, broken nose, broken clavicle. Twelve stitches in his face, and a major concussion. Plus a loose front tooth that they hope to save. So they kept him in, of course.'

He fell silent.

'It's disgusting. They went for his face when he refused to defend himself. He told me he kept thinking he had to protect his hands.

You may not know but Elias is an artist. His hands are his tools.' He paused and looked her.

'Yes, I know,' she said.

'They stole his wallet and his keys.' He shook his head slowly. 'I'm on my way upstairs to call the locksmith and have the locks changed. Just to make sure. Then there are his credit cards and driver's licence. He doesn't want to make a report to the police — don't ask me why. But I can't make him do it. I'm just trying to help him as much as I can.'

She still said nothing, and the silence lingered a little awkwardly between them.

'Well, I'd better get back upstairs then,' he said eventually. He was about to turn and leave but stopped in his tracks.

'Look, it's Tuesday today.' He seemed to hesitate. 'And on Tuesdays Elias and I have dinner together at my place. It's become a habit. I cook something and he comes upstairs for a quick meal. Not today, of course.'

He shrugged, looking a little self-conscious.

'So . . . well, you wouldn't feel like . . .? I've already prepared most of it. Nothing fancy. Quite informal. If it suits you.'

She stood frozen in the half-open doorway.

'Thank you, but I'm afraid that is not possible,' she said quietly. 'Not right now.'

'I see,' he said. 'Another time, perhaps?'

She nodded.

'Well, goodbye, then,' he said. 'I'll let you know how Elias progresses.' He suddenly looked quite formal in an old-fashioned way, as if he would have tipped his hat, had he been wearing one.

He disappeared up the stairs as she closed her door.

———

IT WAS EVENING AND she was sitting in the kitchen with Elias's drawing in front of her when she heard footsteps again.

They definitely stopped outside her door. She looked towards the hallway, listened. After a brief pause she heard him walk away. Why had he not knocked? She was convinced it was Otto again. What did he want now? Had he had a change of mind at the door? She stood up and walked slowly towards the door.

He was no longer there when she opened the door. But on the floor there was a plastic shopping bag. She lifted it cautiously, not sure if she wanted anything to do with it. Then she went back inside with the bag in her hand.

She placed it on the kitchen bench. It smelled vaguely of food, she thought. When she opened it she found a plastic container with what looked like some kind of pale meat patties, broccoli and rice. A small foil-wrapped parcel contained a piece of soft cheese, and loose in the bag there was a peach.

And a book.

She pulled out the book. It was a worn copy of *The Werewolf* by Aksel Sandemose. She had not read it, but she recognised Sandemose's name, of course. And the title. It was one of those books she felt she had always known, had somehow managed to absorb without actually reading.

She sat down at the kitchen table and opened it at random.

> *Was she, too, afraid of losing her identity? Losing it forever, if she was not careful? Perhaps that thing you called personality was not as deeply rooted as you might like to believe? Maybe behind such ideas there lingered the suspicion that you might never have had any identity or personality — that you were living an illusion, a swindle.*

She quickly closed the book and put it down.

11

ELIAS WAS STILL IN hospital. He was found to have internal bleeding — his spleen had burst and he needed surgery. Otto visited him every day, and diligently reported to Elisabeth when he returned home.

She realised she had come to expect the knocks on the door. Perhaps even look forward to them. In the end, she climbed up on a chair and removed the wad of paper from the doorbell.

The food had been eaten and the book read. Her feelings were equally mixed in relation to both. She had had no intention of eating the food, planning to return the bag to where she'd found it. But she had opened the plastic box, tasted a morsel, then eaten the lot. It was fried fish cakes. The flavours were overwhelming. When she got to the peach and bit into the juicy flesh she was overcome by a surge of emotion and had to run to the bathroom and throw up. But the flavour lingered. It was as if something she had managed to suppress was rising back to the surface.

And the book. She couldn't understand why he had given it to her. How he had come to choose that particular book. The inimitable, beautiful Felicia with birds in her hair. And the untamable Erling. Their doomed, yet indestructible love. Why did it move her so? She couldn't stop thinking about it. When she finished she started again, with a pencil in hand. Eventually, the entire fly-leaf was filled with page references. The book spoke to her, but in a language she didn't quite understand. It prompted her to try again and again, hunting for some insight that seemed hidden in the text.

IT HAD BEEN A week of sunny spring days. The air that wafted in through the open bedroom window brought with it the smell of the dry sand on the pavement outside. The nights were no longer soothing stretches of uninterrupted darkness. Her time of peace was diminishing day by day. The visits by the Woman in Green grew less frequent. When she came, she seemed to have dissolved a little. Her visits had begun to lose their focus, as if they were in the process of fading irrevocably.

One day she found a note from Otto on the doormat. 'Off to the supermarket tomorrow. Can I get you anything?' She crumpled it up and threw the ball in the rubbish bin under the sink. But she couldn't erase the offer from her thoughts. Conversely, she found herself thinking of nothing else. Here was her opportunity to avoid the dreaded outing herself, but the ramifications were equally repugnant. She would be accepting another favour.

In the end she did nothing at all.

But the following day she found another bag outside her door. She knew the sound of his footsteps by now, and she heard him stop outside her door. When she checked later, there it was. A bulging plastic shopping bag. At first she just closed the door on it. Muttering under her breath, she paced the apartment for a while.

Then she went back and brought the bag inside.

He had bought her a carton of milk, a loaf of bread, two bananas and two oranges, half a dozen eggs, butter and a piece of hard cheese. She pulled out one item at a time and put them on the bench. Slowly folding the plastic bag, she never once took her eyes off the lined-up food.

'Oh no,' she whispered.

———————

SHE WAS HUNGRY AGAIN. And it hurt. She had fried an egg and eaten it on a slice of bread. The flavours were so intense she had to pause between bites. Afterwards, she felt sick and had to go and lie down.

Now it was rage, not reproach, that the Woman in Green exuded. And for the first time she turned her head and their eyes met.

'I knew it was a mistake, I knew all along. But it just kept coming. One seemingly insignificant incident after another. A package, a book, a drawing. And somehow I was lured in. The light penetrated and I couldn't avoid it. It's like some kind of battle but I don't understand the rules. Whatever I do, I seem to become more entangled. Reeled in against my will. I'm not strong enough to fight it. Not strong enough to resist. But I can't face the thought of leaving this.'

Tears were streaming down her face.

'I'm so very tired.'

———————

THE FOLLOWING DAY SHE tried to calculate how much he would have spent on the food. It was a long time since she'd done any shopping so she had only a dim idea of prices. She took two one-hundred kronor notes from her purse and stuck them in an envelope, but stopped herself as she was about to seal it. She added another note, hoping it would be enough to cover his outlay. She simply could not allow herself to be in his debt. The sense of gratitude was almost unbearable as it was.

She slid the envelope inside a book from one of the boxes in the living room. It was a slim paperback. She hesitated, holding it in her hand. His choice of *The Werewolf* for her indicated a widely read man. This might not be the right book at all. What if he already had it? It wouldn't really serve its purpose, then, would it? But for some reason she had picked this book and she would stick with it. She took a pen from the mug on the table and scribbled on the envelope: *Part 2, chapter 12, last paragraph, last line.*

She stood up abruptly, afraid she might change her mind if she hesitated any longer, ran her fingers through her hair, straightened her t-shirt, and left the apartment.

12

OTTO WAS ON HIS way out for his daily walk when he came across the book. He smiled.

A Book of Common Prayer.

He didn't know it. He thought he recognised the author's name, Joan Didion, but he'd never read anything by her. He had a feeling she was not primarily a novelist. But this was undoubtedly a novel.

He turned to the last page, as he always did with a new book.

I have not been the witness I wanted to be.

Then he turned to the first page and read the first line:

I will be her witness.

It was not until he closed the book that he discovered the envelope. He read the short message written on it, then, without opening the envelope, returned it to the book. He tucked the book into his coat pocket and carried on down the stairs.

There was a pale sun in a white sky but still no real warmth in the air. But he sat down on one of the benches in the churchyard. He opened the book and took out the envelope. His suspicions were confirmed when he opened it. She had given him three hundred kronor. He shook his head. And, added to that, a book.

He lifted his face to the sun and closed his eyes.

SEVERAL MONTHS AFTER MOVING in, Elisabeth Blom had still not unpacked most of her boxes. Something was clearly amiss — he had sensed it the minute he stepped inside her apartment, even though he had been totally focused on helping Elias. He could not help noticing. Just a bed, and in the kitchen a table and two chairs. In the living room just boxes — a lot of boxes.

He'd hardly noticed what the woman herself looked like. Not unattractive, but there was a sense of dejection about her. Just as there was about the apartment. It was not until the following day when he knocked on her door that he had an opportunity to take a good look at her face. She might have struck some people as rude, but he had interpreted it as fear. She hadn't opened the door properly, but held it like a shield between the two of them. And she certainly didn't invite him in.

She was tall and slim, with shoulder-length dark, unkempt hair. He was not good at judging age, but he thought she was in her early fifties, perhaps. A little taller than he was, but then he was quite short for a man — just 1.73 metres. He might even have lost a centimetre or two by now; it was a long time since he'd been measured. In the past it had bothered him that he was not taller. Now, he never thought about it.

She was very pale. And there was that fear in her eyes. What was frightening her so? For a brief moment he'd felt like putting his arms around her. He did nothing of the sort, of course.

He opened the book, turned to chapter 12 and read the last paragraph.

Then he started the book from the beginning.

———————

TWO DAYS LATER CAME the first truly warm day. The day when the city underwent its miraculous annual transformation. It was a Saturday and suddenly there were people everywhere. Windows were cleaned, doors were left open. Bicycles brought out and barbecues cleaned. The balconies hung with flowerboxes holding newly planted geraniums and petunias. The playgrounds filled with cheerful children. The colours seemed brighter, the sounds more intense. Life returned.

Otto stood by the kitchen window looking out. He took a deep breath and smiled to himself, as if he had made a decision, before walking out his door and down the stairs.

He knocked three times and waited. This time she answered the door almost immediately, as though she had heard him coming. She still kept a firm hold on the door handle, but a fleeting smile passed over her face. He decided to take it as an encouragement and cleared his throat.

'I think spring has finally arrived. Or perhaps even summer. Some years there seems to be no time for spring — we are plunged straight into summer. This might be such a year.'

He smiled and went on.

'The church has a little summer café and I think they have opened for the season. I was . . . well, I was thinking of going there for a cup of coffee. Since the weather is so nice. They have tables outside and it's very pleasant.'

He looked at her, and then, resolved to get it out before he lost his nerve, quickly added, 'And I was wondering if you would like to accompany me.'

She opened her mouth but he gestured for her to hear him out.

'It might not be convenient. I understand. It's very short notice. I understand if it's a bad time. If so, perhaps another day? I'd be grateful for the company. I have to admit it's a bit lonely without Elias around.'

She took her time to respond and when she finally did, he quickly returned his gaze to her.

'What time?'

'Oh, whenever,' he said. 'There's no rush. I think they're open all day. For coffee, anyway. Why don't we make it a lunch? He was unable to hide a smile, and looked at his watch, a little self-conscious. 'How about I knock on your door again at eleven-thirty? Would that suit?'

Again, she kept him waiting for her answer.

'All right,' she said finally.

He felt his heart skip a beat. He had not really expected that she would accept.

'Thank you,' he said. 'I'll be back at eleven-thirty, then. And we can talk about the book. I read it with great interest.'

She said nothing further; just gave a short nod and closed the door quietly.

Otto walked up the stairs with light steps.

———————

THEY SAT AT A table that was still in the sun. Otto had hung his coat over the back of his chair and gone inside to place their order. When he returned with the tray, he found Elisabeth sitting with her face to the warm sun. He stopped in his tracks and wondered if he should give her some more time to herself.

I think she's had enough time to herself, he thought. And the sun will shine on her anyway.

She opened her eyes when he approached and helped put the coffee cups, glasses and sandwich plates on the table.

'Ah,' Otto said as he sat down. 'This is the life. Sunshine, coffee and good company. It doesn't get any better than this.'

She smiled briefly, and Otto thought she blushed a little, but she raised her cup and sipped the coffee without comment.

He couldn't take his eyes off her but didn't want to embarrass her by staring. She was beautiful. Without a doubt, a real beauty. But her beauty seemed strangely masked and overshadowed. Almost as if she were intent on hiding it. Dark strong eyebrows, long narrow nose, wide mouth. But it was the eyes that fascinated him. Amber-coloured. They made him think of his mother. The way she had pointed to her eyes and said to him: 'Look here, Otto. Can you see the colour? That is the colour our tea should have. Then it is ready to drink.' And still, every morning when he made his tea, and before he allowed the spoonful of plum jam to slide into the cup, they came to his mind, his mother's amber eyes. Which he had inherited.

Here he was, sitting opposite a woman with those same eyes. For some strange reason it felt like a connection, something that united them. Not that he believed in any kind of reincarnation, or in destiny or any other kind of superstition. He was just overcome with an inexplicable tenderness towards this woman. In that precise moment, with the sun on his back and the smell of grass and coffee in his nose, Otto Vogel was happy. He was not sure if he had ever felt this way before.

They ate their sandwiches in silence. Later, after a refill of coffee, Otto hesitantly began to talk.

'Thank you for the book. I brought it with me . . .' He turned on his chair and struggled to reach his coat pocket, but stopped when Elisabeth shook her head.

'Keep it. I have too many books.'

Otto laughed.

'There was a time when I would have objected to that statement. A time when I thought you could never have too many books. But now I understand what you mean. Perhaps we don't need more books. Perhaps we need to read those we have more carefully.'

He looked out over the churchyard where people were revelling in the sunshine. Sitting on the benches, lying on the grass and strolling along the paths.

'I have been surrounded by books all my life,' he went on. 'My father worked for a book printing house. He wasn't particularly interested in books other than professionally, as products of the printing process. But my mother was. When we moved to Sweden she trained as a school librarian. I can't remember a time when she didn't read. To herself, and to me. So I suppose I was destined to work with books, one way or another. I ended up in a second-hand bookshop, but that's all in the past. Now, all I have to remind me of a life of books are my overfull bookshelves. Not a bad thing but, like you, I have too many. I am grateful for every opportunity to give one away. Especially when I believe it will give pleasure. But I will gratefully place this one among mine for now. One day I might meet someone who needs it.'

He took a sip of coffee.

'I gave Elias books when we first got to know each other. It took him a while to tell me he couldn't really read them. He is severely dyslexic — did you know? It's not that he doesn't have words, or doesn't understand their meanings. He just struggles to extract the meaning of a written word and to formulate his own ideas in written words. So he draws and paints his ideas and thoughts instead. When I realised what was the matter, we started sharing books in a different way. I don't read them, I just tell the stories to him, as I remember them. I think he enjoys it. I certainly do. It has reacquainted me with many old favourites, helped me discover new things in them.'

He smiled again.

'I read the book you gave me with great interest. But I've never found it particularly meaningful to discuss books with other people, so I won't bore you with my interpretation or anything of the sort. I like to keep the reading experience between me and the author.'

He paused briefly, as if reconsidering what he had said.

'Actually it's not even that,' he said eventually. 'The author is of no importance: it's all about the text. Me and the text. Other people's experiences are their own affair. As are the author's intentions. I never read book reviews. But since I started sharing books with Elias, I have come to understand that there are two kinds of reading experience and they are not mutually exclusive.

There is my own private experience, and there is our shared one. So I would like you to know that I read it with great interest, and it made me reflect on aspects of my own life. This makes it a good book in my view. And it is something we share, you and I.'

'I've enjoyed reading the book you gave me, too,' she said. 'I've not read anything by Aksel Sandemose before, but now I have read *Varulven* several times. I may not have recognised myself in it — not in the story itself — but there is an aspect that seems . . . all encompassing. Something fundamentally human. The challenge of living our lives fully. Reading it has made me realise . . .' She left the sentence unfinished.

'That's what good books do, I think,' he said. 'They trigger your own thinking. Make you reflect on your own life. For good or ill. There is comfort and wisdom to be had from good books.'

The conversation turned to Elias. Or rather, Otto talked about Elias. He told Elisabeth it looked likely Elias would be released from hospital the following week.

'I thought we should celebrate with dinner at my place as soon as he is up to it.'

He cocked his head and looked at Elisabeth.

But he received no response. She closed her eyes and lifted her face to the sun.

'We'll have to ask him, of course. Mostly he just talks about getting back to his project. You know, the one . . .' He bit his lip. Of course she knew nothing of Elias's project.

'Well, he is always working on something,' he said vaguely. 'He's actually quite a well-known cartoonist — except that word is a little misleading. Elias is much more than a cartoonist. He's an artist, and his works are novels where the pictures are so expressive that the words seem almost secondary. The graphic novel is a genre that never interested me before. I'm not sure I even knew it existed and I doubt that it did in my day, when I had my shop. There were illustrated classics, of course. But what Elias does is different: an artform in its own right. And now I am completely hooked. A lot of it is rubbish, of course. But that's the case in all genres, I suppose. Elias is one of the best in his. It's not just that he's a very talented artist, but his stories truly move you. He cannot form the words but the story is in his head and is released through his hands.'

'Do the stories have no words at all?' Elisabeth asked.

'Well, yes, they do. Ever since he started, he has worked with a childhood friend, Maja Fredriksson, who is an author. They work almost telepathically, as far as I understand it. Elias tells the story in his drawings and Maja adds the words. The end result is extraordinary. I have all their books upstairs. You're most welcome to read them.'

He looked up.

'More coffee?' He pointed at her cup.

She nodded and handed it to him. He left to get both cups refilled.

'Here I am talking away,' he said as he sat down again. 'I apologise if I am boring you.'

She shook her head.

'He gave me one of his drawings just before the assault,' she said slowly. She had a dark voice and she articulated the words so clearly that he wondered if she might be an actress, or perhaps a newsreader. It was a beautiful voice and he heard every word, even though she spoke quietly.

'And before that another picture, a strange ink drawing that I could not make any sense of. It was tucked inside a book I had given him as a thank you for a favour. He returned it with the drawing inside. I didn't know it was his own work. That first one, it's . . .' She seemed to be searching for the right word. 'Well, it's fascinating, but it's just beyond me to interpret it. At first I thought it had ended up in the book by mistake. But then I saw he had written a short message in the margin. It took me a while to understand it referred to the book. I realised he must have meant for me to have it after all, but I was none the wiser as to what it meant.'

She took a deep breath and continued.

'Then he gave me the second one. A completely different kind of drawing: a bird against a background that looks like slushy snow. The bird looks so real, so alive. Or actually half dead. Scrawny and broken. But so skilfully drawn I thought I could see its little chest heave as the bird gasped for air.'

She stopped, looking a little embarrassed.

Otto made a gesture to encourage her to continue.

'I can't explain why it moved me so much. Such a simple image — just a few black brushstrokes. But I guess that is exactly the challenge: to make just the right strokes. Like finding the right words, the right expression for what you want to say. I know nothing about art, but I can see that he is talented.'

She looked down and ran her hand over the table in front of her, mumbling something that Otto didn't quite catch. She lifted her gaze again.

'I've been thinking about what you told me. How he tried to protect his hands. It upsets me every time I think about it. Not being able to defend himself . . .'

Otto nodded slowly.

The church bells above their heads struck two o'clock.

Elisabeth jumped, as if abruptly reminded where she was. Otto thought she looked frightened again. Or at least worried.

'Perhaps it's time for us to wander back?' he said.

She stood up quickly — so quickly that the chair fell over behind her. Otto went to pick it up and their eyes met as they bent down simultaneously.

'I'm so grateful for this little chat. It will give me pleasure for several days,' Otto said. 'Thank you for keeping me company.'

She said nothing, just bowed her head a little and started to walk down the slope.

Down on the pathway she stumbled, and Otto caught her hand and put her arm under his own, with his other hand resting reassuringly on her arm.

She let him, but her arm was weightless under his.

13

SHE HAD CLOSED THE door behind her and stood leaning against it with her eyes closed. Her cheeks were burning from the sun and her breathing was laboured. When she finally opened her eyes again she saw her own hallway with frightening clarity. Every detail was exposed, as if stage lit. Bright rays of sunshine had found their way inside from the kitchen window and streaked the floorboards. There were no traces of human life here. Nothing indicating her own presence.

She took off her shoes and walked slowly into the kitchen, seeing it, too, as though for the first time. The pile of mail on the table. A dirty plate and cutlery in the sink and a glass on the bench. But it could have been days, months — years, even — since someone had set foot in here.

She walked to the table and picked up the picture of the bird. She considered it for a moment, then took it with her to the living room. There, she kneeled down, placed the picture on the floor and opened one of the boxes. She groped inside until she found a roll of double-sided tape.

In the bedroom she tore off a couple of strips of tape and attached them to the back of the painting. Taking care to get it straight, she stuck the picture on the empty wall facing her bed. She ran her palm carefully over the picture to make sure it was stuck properly to the wall.

She stepped back, never taking her eyes off the picture, and sank down on the bed.

WHEN SHE WOKE IT was early evening but still not quite dark. That time of year was over. The soothing darkness was gone and the nights would gradually become lighter.

The room felt cold and she realised she had left the window open. Even though she was not aware of any meeting with the Woman in Green, her memory lingered in the room. It obscured the bird on the wall.

Elisabeth stood up and closed the window, but she could still smell the spring evening. As she gazed through the dirty window pane the events of earlier in the day felt completely unreal. Had she really ventured outside? Sat in the sun with that man? Sipped coffee and eaten a sandwich? Conversed, even? The memory felt like a wedge of light driven into her soft darkness. She couldn't understand why she had agreed to go. It would have been so easy just to close the door. Then she could have remained blissfully unaware of the bright spring sunshine outside. As it was, everything was irrevocably altered.

She went to the living room and kneeled down by the boxes. She began to tear open the flaps of first one, then another, and another, until all the boxes had been opened. There were twelve in all. All but one containing books. She pulled a few books from the first box. Why had she brought all these? She put them on the floor and retrieved a thick hardback book from the box. Then she sat herself properly on the floor and opened its pages.

14

HE HAD BEEN AWAY for a little over three weeks but it felt like a very long time when he stepped back inside his apartment. Otto held his arm under his. Elias didn't need it, but he allowed his arm to stay put.

'I've cleaned a little. Vacuumed and so on. Aired it. Funny how quickly the air goes stale with nobody living in a place. But I haven't moved anything, I promise.' Otto glanced towards the window. 'I guess I should have cleaned the windows, but I drew the line there. I haven't even cleaned my own! The dirt is horribly visible in the sharp spring light.'

Elias gently let go of Otto's arm and paced the room, as if refamiliarising himself. He put down the drawing pad he was carrying and looked at Otto.

'It's good to be home. Thank you for everything you've done for me. For being there all this time. For doing this . . .' He swept his arm to take in the whole room.

Otto looked pleased.

'No more similar dramas, please! I'm not a young man and

there's a limit to what I can take. Look after yourself, will you?'

Elias sat down at the desk.

'How do you feel?' Otto asked.

'Fine. Absolutely fine. I can still feel the ribs, but it's getting better.'

'You never did report it to the police, did you?'

Elias shrugged.

'What's the point? It was dark — I hardly saw them until they were all over me. And I was completely focused on trying to protect myself. These things happen all the time. The police couldn't care less. They'd probably think it was my own fault.'

'What do you mean your own fault? Shouldn't you be able to walk the streets without expecting to be assaulted?'

'Perhaps people like me have to expect it.'

'People like you? What do you mean?'

'Well, you know . . .'

Elias stood up abruptly. 'I've started drawing again,' he said as he walked to the table and opened his drawing pad.

'You're changing the subject on me.' Otto was frowning.

'Exactly.'

Elias smiled a lopsided smile.

'I promised that you would get to see it when I felt ready to share it. Here it is.' He motioned to the armchair and handed Otto the drawing pad.

Otto laid it across his knees and opened it carefully. He sat in silence, slowly lifting one leaf after another. There were sixty pages all in all, and about two-thirds were finished.

Elias walked to the window and opened it.

'I think the whole story is taking shape,' he said with his back to Otto. 'It's a simple story — not at all like my earlier ones. It's like this story has a life of its own. I don't feel I'm totally in control. But I can see it quite clearly. It's revealing itself little piece by little piece. I still don't know how it will end.'

Eventually Otto closed the pad, exhaled and rubbed his chin. He said nothing for quite a while. Then he cleared his throat, keeping his eyes on the pad on his lap. He ran his palms over the cover, searching for the right words.

'This, Elias . . . this is something very special. I'm not sure what to say. You know I don't know much about art. I suppose all I can say is that I am deeply moved.' He lifted his glasses and pinched his nose for a moment. 'Utterly, utterly moved.'

'Do you really mean that?'

Otto looked up.

'Of course I mean it. You know me better than that, don't you? You know I would never say something I didn't mean.'

Elias blushed a little.

'That lonely little bird. In that icy cold snow. Makes you wonder if it will survive.' Otto paused. 'This . . . this is simply the best work you have ever done, Elias. And even I can understand what it is about, I think. You can see how everything is balancing on the edge, so very fragile. It's as if I can see the images move. It's . . . well, it's simply astonishing. And, as you said, it's impossible to tell how it will end. It could go either way. I can't wait to find out, and yet at the same time I don't want to know. That little bird on the wet snow, so completely broken. There's hardly any life left in it at all, but you sense that it has a strong will to live. Yet also a longing to give in. Will it accept those cupped hands? The help offered? You make us understand the formidable fight it faces.'

Otto closed the pad with great care.

'It's not just a bird, though, is it?'

Elias shook his head.

'No. It's not just a bird.'

Otto asked nothing further.

'I think we have cause for a celebration. Firstly, because you are back home. Secondly, because spring is here. And finally because your project has advanced this far. So very exciting!'

Elias smiled. 'Dinner at your place?'

'Great minds! A spring supper at my place. And I think we should invite Elisabeth, your neighbour. It's thanks to her that you're here today. Who knows what would have happened if she'd not heard you? Besides, I think she needs to get out.'

'Do you really think she'll want to?' Elias looked sceptical.

Otto shrugged.

'It's worth a try. If we ask the right way she may accept. Besides, you do want to thank her in person, don't you? That's a good excuse to invite her.'

'I haven't had much luck in communicating with her so far. What do I do if she doesn't open the door? Shout through the letter slot again?'

'You might be pleasantly surprised. I don't mind what day we do it but let's not wait too long. You probably need to take it easy for a while. Collect yourself. But then, any time.'

'I feel quite collected, thanks,' Elias said with a smile. 'I think I can manage dinner at your place. I'll knock on her door and we'll see what she says.'

'Try the doorbell. It works now.'

15

SHE SAT CROSS-LEGGED ON the living-room floor surrounded by her opened boxes. They contained all her worldly goods: everything she had chosen to bring with her. Why all these books? Because they were all that remained? The only tangible proof of what had been? And all that was absolutely hers.

She reached into the nearest box and took out a handful of books, then another. She worked with increasing speed and soon dozens of books lay in piles around her.

Inside the fourth box she found what she'd been searching for. Not that she had been aware of searching for anything at all. But as soon as her hands closed around the thick sheaf of paper, she knew this was what she was after. What she had really packed when she boxed up all those books. As though she had wanted to cushion it. Hide it.

She slowly lifted out the papers.

She stretched out her legs, placed the pile on her lap and removed the rubber band that held the pages together. Her hand riffled the pages while her unseeing eyes rested on the cover sheet.

It looked so insignificant. Just a pile of cheap copy paper. Yet it had determined her entire life. Or rather, finished everything she had considered her life to be.

The sobs came without forewarning. Broke through from deep inside, completely impossible to restrain. She gave in and allowed them to come forth. She howled and bawled and moaned. She held the sheaf of paper close to her chest and rocked to and fro.

When her grief finally subsided she remained where she was on the floor, completely still. She lowered the papers and began slowly leafing through them. Turning one sheet at a time. She was not reading. There was no need to do that — she knew it all by heart, including the pencil notes in the margin. Still, she turned the pages slowly, one by one.

After she turned the last page she rose stiffly, clutching the manuscript to her chest. Once on her feet she looked around, as if surprised to find herself where she was.

With a strength she had not been aware of possessing, she threw the papers across the room. The sheets fell all over the floor.

She was standing barefoot surrounded by books and strewn paper when the doorbell rang.

She stiffened. Held her hands to her face. Oh, no. Oh, no.

The doorbell rang again.

She stepped over the books, slipping a little on a piece of paper, and stepped into the hallway.

She assumed it must be Otto, probably on his way to the supermarket. He had taken to calling in every time he went shopping, which seemed to be most days.

She stood eyeing the door.

When it rang a third time she jumped, even though she had been standing on alert, expecting it.

She dried her tears with the back of her hand and took a deep breath. Then cautiously opened the door.

It was not Otto. It was Elias.

For the first time she saw what he looked like. Tall, but that she knew. Dark curly hair. A red scar ran over one eye. His eyes looked grey, with strong brows.

He smiled a little awkwardly, but it was a warm smile. It was a very attractive man of about thirty who stood before her. Yet he exuded a kind of insecurity, at odds with his looks. His smile was contagious.

'I hope I'm not disturbing you. I just wanted to say . . . well, tell you that I'm back home. And thank you for your help. If you hadn't heard me, I'm not sure I would be here today. I think you saved my life.'

She shook her head.

'Yes, you did. So, well . . . I want you to know that I am so very grateful. And I'd like to give you this.' He held out a rolled-up paper. 'It's just one of my drawings. Nothing special.'

She reached out and took it.

'Thank you.' She pulled the door to, as if to end the conversation.

But he showed no sign of leaving.

'We were wondering . . . well, Otto and I thought we should celebrate with a small dinner party up at Otto's. It was his idea. We both think it would be great if you could join us. Maybe tomorrow?'

When she said nothing, he continued.

'Feel free to suggest another day. We're not exactly overbooked, the two of us.' He smiled a little.

'No, I don't think so . . .' she said, shaking her head.

His disappointment was obvious. She bit her lip and looked down.

'But thank you, anyway. It was a kind thought.'

'What if I tell you that it would mean a lot to me? Also, I would really like to talk to you. About that.' He pointed to the paper roll.

She looked at it with surprise, and then at him.

'To me?'

'Yes, to you. That's what I want more than anything else right now.'

She made no reply.

'You don't need to stay long. And it's just the three of us. I know it would make Otto happy, too. He's a little lonely, I think.'

She kept her gaze lowered, still saying nothing.

'You would cheer us up. Both of us.'

'Me?' She snorted, a short, dry little laugh filled with genuine surprise.

'Yes, that's right. If you want to think about it, I can come back later.'

He made to leave.

'Thank you. I will be there. Tomorrow. What time?'

'Oh, it doesn't really matter, knowing Otto. How about five-ish? I can ring your bell when I leave and we can go upstairs together. How's that?'

She nodded.

And with that he left.

16

NOW THAT IT WAS decided, he felt nervous. And ridiculous for feeling nervous. It had been his idea, and it was just an ordinary little dinner.

He had taken out the few cookbooks he owned and sat at the kitchen table flicking through them. Should they have an entrée? If so, what? Were there things she didn't eat? Some people didn't eat fish. Or shellfish. Or red meat. Chicken, perhaps? Chicken might be a safe bet — most people ate chicken. Unless they were vegetarian. But she was not, that he knew. She had eaten a ham sandwich at the café.

It was spring, and if the weather kept up it would be a lovely evening. But the spring foods were mostly not yet available — like new potatoes, asparagus, strawberries. Imported, yes, but that was not the same.

He realised he was not just nervous, he was also filled with a childish anticipation. His cheeks felt hot to the touch. It was as if his whole body was several degrees hotter than normal and the blood flowed more quickly. If it had not been a ridiculous thought, he would have said he felt young. Excited in a way he couldn't remember having been for a very long time. If ever.

Chicken it would be. And he'd have to see what vegetables were available. Dessert? Would tinned rosehip soup be too ordinary? With vanilla ice-cream and those little almond biscuits? He liked that. There would be no cooking involved and therefore no risk of disaster.

Now, the entrée. What did people have for entrées? He'd forgotten. Or possibly never known. It had been such a long time since he'd had a three-course dinner. Prawn cocktail? No, too risky and too complicated. She may not be able to eat that. Melon and smoked ham? That sounded a little spring-like. He decided to go for that. Easy, and again, no cooking involved.

What to drink? Champagne? Yes, definitely. They would have champagne. There was a lot to celebrate. Some red wine. Or white? Or both? Beer for Elias, perhaps? He was not sure if Elias drank red wine. Cognac? Probably not. He didn't want to overdo it — that would look . . . well, ridiculous. There it was again, that word. Yes, he might be ridiculous. Perhaps the whole idea was ridiculous. It didn't matter. He would embrace this feeling of anticipation. Allow the blood to flow and his cheeks to blush.

To his surprise, he found himself whistling as he pulled on his coat. He strode confidently down the stairs and out the main entrance.

17

IT FELT VERY DIFFERENT from the usual Tuesday dinners. It was not Tuesday, of course, but that was not the reason.

Elias stood in front of the bathroom mirror. He had showered and shaved. Brushed his teeth. Even flossed. He examined himself critically. The scar over his eye shone bright red. The surgeon had said it would fade over time but he didn't mind if it didn't. He was just so grateful that he'd been able to save his hands. He held them up to the mirror. Clenched and unclenched them several times, as if to test them. Leaning closer to the glass, he locked eyes with his mirror image.

He had tried not to dwell on the attack, focusing instead on getting well as fast as possible. Even if he didn't know who his attackers were, he knew *what* they were. He'd encountered them all his life, in different shapes and forms. Pushing, kicking, calling names. Ripping up his drawings. Tearing his clothes. Making the walk to school a dreaded daily torture. And there was Otto insisting that he report the attack to the police.

He smiled at the idea. There was no police protection against this. There was no protection at all for people like him.

He left the bathroom and pulled on his jeans and a clean white t-shirt. He was ready.

At the front door he stopped in his tracks. He returned to the living room and picked up his drawing pad.

It was as though she had been waiting just inside her door, because he had hardly removed his hand from the doorbell when she appeared. When he saw what she was wearing he laughed.

'Great minds think alike,' he said, pointing to her jeans and white t-shirt.

'Yes, or we are short of options. I know I am,' she said.

She'd cut her hair. It was shorter, definitely, but very crudely chopped, as if done with a blunt pair of scissors. She'd done it herself, he decided. And for some reason the thought moved him. She had a slim book in her hand.

'Ready?'

She stepped out and closed the door behind her. He walked ahead of her up the stairs. All the way they could smell food cooking, and when Otto opened the door the aromas billowed out into the stairwell. He looked a little flustered, but his smile was wide and welcoming as he invited them in.

He steered them down the hall.

'I had intended cleaning the whole place but I ran out of time so only the kitchen is presentable, really. Do you mind if we eat in there?'

He gestured towards the kitchen but Elisabeth stopped in front of the floor-to-ceiling bookcase that ran the entire length of the hall. There were further piles of books on the floor, and she could see the opening to the living room with more bookcases.

'I know,' Otto said. 'It's ridiculous. But for a large part of my life all those books have sustained me. In more ways than one. And when I moved here I couldn't bear to leave any behind. Lately I've been trying to rid myself of them gradually, one by one. But I like to give them good new homes, not just discard them. I like to think they could give someone the kind of pleasure they have given me.'

'And here I am adding to your burden,' Elisabeth said, holding out the book she had brought with her.

'Ah,' he said, sounding pleasantly surprised. 'Another one that is unknown to me.' He turned the book in his hands and opened it at the last page. He chuckled a little as he read:

And the porcelains were bits of old crockery that simply had to go.

'Another collector of sorts?'

'Yes,' she said, and held out her hand for the book. She flicked through the pages until she found what she was looking for.

Things, I reflected, are tougher than people. Things are the changeless mirror in which we watch ourselves disintegrate. Nothing is more ageing than a collection of works of art.

She closed the book and gave it back to Otto.

'*Utz* by Bruce Chatwin,' he said. 'It's a novel, isn't it? Am I right in thinking he's better known for his travel books?'

Elisabeth nodded.

'Well, I look forward to reading it. And since you have added to my book collection I have to ask you to take one of mine when you leave tonight. Now, let's eat!'

He led them into the kitchen and pulled out a chair for Elisabeth.

Elias sat down opposite her.

'I thought we should begin with a glass of champagne,' Otto said, opening the fridge. 'We have several reasons to celebrate, and celebrations call for champagne, don't they? Not that I'm an expert — quite the opposite, I'm afraid. Only tasted it once in my life. I have a feeling it will taste much better tonight.'

He began to remove the wires from the cork.

'Do you want some help?' Elias rose from the chair. 'Not that I am an expert either, but—'

That was as far as he got before the cork hit the ceiling with a loud bang. Otto looked up and saw that it had left a small mark.

'I should have had many more of those by now. Signs of celebrations and parties with good friends.'

'Well, it's a start,' Elisabeth said, and it seemed to take both men by surprise. Otto tried to disguise his by attending to filling the three glasses. Elias stood to take one of the glasses from the bench and handed it to Elisabeth.

They raised their glasses in a toast.

'Don't worry, I'm not going to make a speech,' said Otto. 'I just want to say that I do hope so, Elisabeth. I do hope it's a start. The beginning of our friendship.' He nodded to her and held up his glass. 'Here's to us. To celebrations. To friendship. And to good health of course.'

They toasted, then tasted the champagne.

'Ah, yes,' said Otto. He looked down into his glass and for a moment he seemed preoccupied. He took another sip. 'I knew it would be better this time. Much better.'

THE FOOD WAS A great success and the conversation flowed easily, even if Elisabeth didn't contribute much other than nodding and smiling. They talked about books. Music. And food. The meal over, Otto and Elisabeth sat drinking tea and Elias had a bottle of beer in front of him. He kept slowly turning it.

'I've brought my drawing pad,' he said tentatively, 'but I'm not sure if this is the right occasion . . .'

'I can't imagine a better occasion,' said Otto. 'Get it!'

Elias went out and returned with the large pad under his arm. Otto moved their mugs to make room on the table. He pulled his chair up to sit beside Elisabeth. Elias stood beside them, lifting one page at a time.

'I am thinking of it as a book. Like my earlier ones, in a way. But at the same time totally different.' He kept holding on to the pad as if he wasn't quite sure he wanted to share it. Then he placed it on the table.

'These are only the full-page illustrations. I have smaller ones, too, but I didn't bring them. It's difficult to explain my thinking,' he said, 'and it may not be easy to get the whole story from just these.'

'Can we not just look?' said Elisabeth unexpectedly. Her eyes were on the first picture.

Elias watched her for his cues to turn a leaf. She seemed oblivious and never returned his gaze. Some of the pictures were more like sketches, but most looked to be completed. The room was silent. When Elias finally closed the pad, Elisabeth looked up.

'Can I see them once more?' she asked quietly.

Elias started again from the beginning.

'It was so damned lucky they didn't get at your hands,' Otto said finally.

Elisabeth said nothing. When Otto threw her a quick glance he noticed she had tears in her eyes.

He stood up.

'More tea, Elisabeth?' he asked.

There was no reply.

She turned towards the half-open window and sat absolutely still.

Elias picked up the pad and returned it to the hallway. He exchanged a quick questioning glance with Otto, who gave a brief shrug, looking equally puzzled.

Otto set Elisabeth's refilled tea mug in front of her and placed his hand lightly on her shoulder.

She didn't move and didn't seem to have noticed the tea.

'I think it's time for me to get back downstairs,' Elias said from the doorway. 'Do you want to come, Elisabeth, or would you like to stay a little longer?'

She said nothing but rose slowly.

'Thank you,' she said and held out her hand. Otto took it between both of his. Then he pulled her towards him and gave her a hug.

He turned to Elias and hugged him, too. 'Thank you both for coming.' He glanced up at the ceiling. 'It does feel like a start, doesn't it?'

Elisabeth's gaze rested on the two men where they stood in the kitchen, lit only by the gentle light from the glass chandelier over the table.

She nodded and followed them into the hallway.

'Now, don't forget to pick a book,' said Otto.

Elisabeth walked along the bookshelf, hands clasped behind her back. Every so often she slowed down, but she didn't pull out any book. When she reached the end of the hall she slowly walked back, eyes intent on the rows of books. Finally she stopped and pulled out a hardback volume.

'You may not want to part with this one,' she said, and held it out to Otto.

'You're doing me a favour, Elisabeth. There is nothing on these shelves that I would not like to give you. There are a small number of books that for different reasons have a special meaning for me. I keep those by my bed. All of these I would like to find good homes for.'

'Thank you,' said Elisabeth and followed Elias out into the stairwell, book in hand.

———

OTTO HAD DONE THE dishes and sat at the table reading. The cool night air wafted through the window. It was a slim little book but he took his time, savouring the words. Every now and then he lifted his eyes from the book, focusing for a moment on the fragrance that was drifting in. He took a deep breath, wondering if perhaps the old bird-cherry tree in the courtyard was about to bloom. He didn't think so — it was too early — but there was certainly a new sweetness to the air.

When he finally closed the book he sensed that the night had turned and it was already morning. He got up and turned off the lamp. For a moment he stood by the window, his hands on the sill. Yes, there was a subtle change to the colour of the sky. It looked as if it were lit from behind, intensely saturated blue, paler across the rooftops and darker higher up. He took another deep breath, and just as he was about to turn away he heard the first tune. He sank down on a chair and closed his eyes.

The blackbird was back.

The four walls framing the courtyard enhanced the sound as it lifted towards the sky. The jubilant song was amplified in the confined space, every note exquisitely defined.

Otto folded his arms on the table and rested his head on them. He closed his eyes and soon he was fast asleep.

18

SHE STEPPED INSIDE THE unlit apartment. For the first time since she moved in, she had something to compare it to.

The apartment above was light and warm. She could imagine Otto busy in the kitchen. Perhaps he was listening to some music. During dinner he had talked a lot about music and it transpired he was interested and knowledgeable. He had played that wonderful trio. She couldn't remember when she had last played music. Here, she had neither a radio nor a stereo. She had not even bothered to open her laptop. Perhaps it would no longer be possible to charge it.

She went into the bedroom, opened the window and sank down on the bed. It was dark and quiet outside, but the darkness was no longer absolute. Not even in the middle of the night. There was light behind the dark sky now. The silence no longer felt total either — more of a breathing space. A brief pause.

She lay back on the bed and pulled a corner of the blanket over her. Then she turned on the reading light. Now she could see the drawing on the wall, and for a split-second she thought she saw the bird move. Open its wings ever so softly. And again the image brought tears to her eyes. She couldn't — or wouldn't — think about why it moved her so. Elias had said he wanted to talk to her about it. She couldn't imagine why. She had nothing to offer. Just her tears.

She had placed Otto's book on the box by the bed. Strindberg's *Inferno*. But she didn't feel like reading. Yet she was not really sleepy. Physically exhausted, maybe, as if she had done a lot of heavy manual work, but with her head full of images and impressions of the evening. She examined them one by one, afraid that she might have said or done something inappropriate.

It was a long time before she dropped off to sleep.

———

SHE HAD KNOWN IT was wrong. The moment she accepted the invitation she knew. When she cut her hair and searched the boxes for something to wear, a part of her was watching, smiling smugly and shaking its head at the folly of her efforts. She had come such a long way towards the peace she craved, and now she was risking it all for an evening with two people she hardly knew.

And now here she was, more indebted than ever. The kindness showered on her clung to her, weighed her down. Dinner. Music. Books. And then the damned drawings. It hurt to look at them but it was impossible not to. This young man had somehow worked his way inside her head with his images. Now that they were there, there was no way to get rid of them. They were all stuck in her head and couldn't be erased. There they were, as clear as the one on her wall.

The Woman in Green looked straight at her, but she was further away than usual. This time there was no reproach in her expression. No, it was worse. It was pity. She made no sound, but the message was utterly clear.

'You fool. You are moving away, Elisabeth. And you will end

up alone again. You know the dangers. The devastating pain connected with life out there. Are you sure that is what you want?'

'No!' she screamed. 'That's not what I want! I just wanted a little . . .'

The Woman in Green slowly shook her head. Her sadness was infinite.

'There is no such thing, Elisabeth. You know that. You can't just have a little life. It is life. Or no life.'

The room grew slowly lighter and with the light the Woman in Green faded.

Elisabeth sat up in bed. She realised she was still fully dressed. Just as she was about to stand up, the sound entered the room. The first few notes of a blackbird's song. It was not very loud, perhaps coming from the courtyard on the other side of the building. But it was absolutely pure and clear, a jubilant song.

Brimming with the joy of life.

19

ELIAS WAS WAITING FOR Maja to arrive. He knew there was no use asking her to reconsider the job, and he hoped he would be able to refrain from even trying. But he still wanted her view on the drawings, wanted to know what she saw in them.

He had all the finished images in the computer, but now he was laying out the large originals on the floor, in order. There were twelve of them, intended as full-page images. The smaller ones were still in the drawing pads, as well as in the computer.

This was very different from any book he had created before. Firstly, he had never used full-page illustrations. Secondly, he had never worked this fast. Or this single-mindedly.

He stood up and viewed the images from above. There was nothing he wanted to change. He let his gaze wander from one picture to the next, hearing the story in his head. The question was, would anybody else hear it?

There was still a lot of work to do, but never before had he had such a complete picture in his head of the whole book. Every image seemed so obvious even before he put pen to paper.

The doorbell rang.

He had known Maja most of his life. She was almost a part of him. His best friend and for a long time his protector. She was the closest thing he had to family. There was nobody he trusted more — her judgement meant everything. He felt his heart race.

'Okay, let me see them now!' she said, and gave him a quick peck on the cheek.

Her eyes on the drawings, she slowly removed her jacket and dropped it on the floor. She said nothing, and Elias stood behind her, nervously chewing his lip.

Finally she turned around and, to Elias's amazement, she had tears in her eyes. She threw her arms around his neck.

'Oh, Elias, this, this is . . . my God, I don't know what to say! Me, Maja Fredriksson, lost for words!' She was crying and laughing at the same time. 'It's a whole life. It starts with that broken bird . . . but it's not about a bird, is it?'

He released himself from her arms, holding on to her shoulders.

Then he started crying, too. He pulled her to him and lifted her off her feet. They both laughed and snivelled, turning in circles, embracing. When they let go of each other they stood side by side, eyes on the images in front of them on the floor.

'I knew you would see it,' he said quietly, taking her hand. 'Yes, I'm trying to tell a life story. It started just with that glimpse of a woman. Who took on the shape of my bird. But I just couldn't stop myself.'

He shrugged, blushing.

'I'm not sure I can explain it, Maja, but this is what I have always wanted to experience. This sense of being completely sure of where I am going, what I want to achieve. With this project I know exactly.'

She nodded.

'In a way, I'm glad I'm not writing the words to this. It's *sooo* beyond my ability, Elias. This is . . . well, it's poetry. And I'm not a poet.'

'Can you hear it, though?'

'Yes, I can hear it. Not as words, but as feelings. The absolutely terrible loneliness in the first pictures. The fear of being abandoned.

The desperation. The temptation of giving in, letting go. The tug between life and death. Love and hatred. Revenge. But through it all the inextinguishable longing for love.'

She paused.

'There you go, Elias. You can hear how I'm struggling to express what I see, can't you? I can feel it, see it in your pictures, but this needs such special words. As precise as your images. As evocative. As delicate. I am not sure there are such words, Elias. I certainly don't have them.'

'Perhaps you're right. Perhaps there are no words for these pictures.'

Maja cocked her head and looked at him.

'Are you sure it matters?'

Elias didn't respond straight away but stood pondering Maja's question.

Finally he nodded.

'Yes, there must be words. Whatever those words might be. And wherever I might find them. But they must exist. I need to hear them.'

'Well, if that's the case, you will find them. Sooner or later. It's strange how what you really need does come to you eventually, often in the most unexpected way. You just have to be alert. Your words are out there somewhere, and you will find them.' She placed her hand on his cheek.

'Must run.' She picked up her jacket, gave Elias a quick peck.

'I hope you can come to my party on Whitsun Eve,' she said over her shoulder as she walked towards the door. 'The usual routine: same crowd, same food, same place. Mum's allotment garden at Tanto. Fingers crossed it won't rain.'

With that she disappeared out the door.

20

OTTO WOKE EARLIER THAN usual. He had finally made the effort and done a thorough spring clean of his apartment. Not the kind of spring clean he remembered his mother doing — washing ceilings and walls, airing all clothes. But still, as he placed his feet on the floor he could feel that it was clean. The early morning light had free access through the clean windows, and as he opened the kitchen window the fresh morning air filled the room. He couldn't decide what exactly the air smelt like, but he inhaled it with gratitude.

He decided to make proper tea, not use the tea bags. He savoured every mouthful, and ate his piece of toast slowly and mindfully. It looked to be a beautiful early summer day. A day to spend outdoors.

Eva had liked the outdoors, in her way. When the weather was good, she liked to sit in the shade in the small back garden, cigarette in hand, vacantly staring into the distance. He had often been tempted to ask what she was thinking but he never did. Now, he could see her clearly in his mind, her beautiful legs elegantly crossed and her small, perfect feet in dainty mules. When they went on holiday she loved strolling along the beach-front promenades but he never once saw her swim. It was as if she liked it best when there was a distance between herself and the world. She liked observing, never participating. On the few occasions he had insisted on swimming, she had always stayed safely out of reach, under a parasol at a beach café, her blonde hair unruffled and dark sunglasses hiding her eyes.

He put his mug in the sink and went to have a shower.

OTTO DID NOT CARE much about his appearance. He'd never felt himself attractive in any way and he had never dressed to be noticed. He had no interest in clothes but he did care about quality. Since he stopped working he had no need for much more than a few easy-care shirts, a few pairs of trousers and a couple of jerseys. But now he stood in front of the wardrobe in his underwear suddenly acutely aware of a lack of choice. The colours were all subdued: navy, grey and tan. He pulled on a pair of grey trousers. He knew that polo shirts were the thing to wear in summer but he didn't own any. He observed the row of near-identical long-sleeved cotton shirts and sighed. Eventually he picked a white shirt with grey stripes.

Shoes. It might be warm enough for sandals. He stared down at his feet. Milky white, the blue veins visible. The nails had a tinge of yellow, he thought. An old man's feet. Could he wear socks with the sandals? No, he'd read that that was an absolute fashion no-no. So, what else did he have to choose from? Black lace-up shoes: three very similar pairs of good quality. But wrong — completely wrong on a day like today. A pair of what he thought were called boat shoes. Not that he had ever sailed. He'd bought them on recommendation for his first visit to Ekholmen but he'd only ever worn them there, on the island. They would have to do. They were brown, not the best match with the trousers, but who cared? Why was he even thinking about it?

He stuck his feet into the shoes — without socks, as he had seen other people do. It felt strange and he took a couple of steps around the room. No, socks it would have to be, as usual.

He returned to the bathroom and dabbed his cheeks with eau de cologne. It was a good one, he knew. He'd started using it long before it had become fashionable, after Eva bought him a bottle in Rome. He'd been astonished when she told him how much it cost. But he liked it. Eva claimed it would make him irresistible. He'd never seen any sign that it worked with her, but he had had the odd compliment from other women over the years. It had become his one luxury. Not counting the books, of course. Every time they returned to Rome he would buy a couple of bottles. Now, you could buy them anywhere.

He added another splash.

HE RANG THE DOORBELL, and for a moment he felt like running back upstairs. But there was no time — she opened the door almost immediately. She was in her dressing gown and her hair was tousled.

'I am sorry, did I wake you up?' he said.

She shook her head.

'No, not at all.'

'It's just, well, I woke up really early, and it's such a beautiful morning. I, well, I just felt that it would be nice to go for a long walk. Or at least longer than usual.'

She made no response.

'One place I like very much, especially this time of the year, is Fåfängan. Have you been there?'

She shook her head.

'So, I wondered if you felt like coming with me? We could have coffee or lunch up there. Mostly I like it because of the view.'

She definitely looked negative, he thought.

'It's not far, but once you're up there you feel like you're in another world.' He cocked his head to one side. 'I think you'll like it. And I'd like it very much if you would come. I'd really enjoy the company. It's not the same looking at the view by yourself.'

She cleared her throat. 'I'm not really . . .'

'Please,' he said, immediately realising how pathetic he sounded. 'You must forgive me for being so forward. I didn't intend to come across like that. It's just that it's the first real summer day and it would be nice to somehow mark it.'

She nodded slowly. 'It's kind of you to ask me, but I'm not really in any state to go for a walk. Not right now.'

'I have all the time in the world. You tell me when would be a good time.'

'What time is it now?'

He looked at his watch.

'Nine-thirty. How about I come back at eleven?'

She seemed to hesitate.

'I'll be ready.'

———————

THEY WALKED ALONG TJÄRHOVSGATAN in a companion-able silence. Otto had offered his arm and Elisabeth had taken it. They crossed the small park at Tjärhovsplan and continued over Folkungagatan. There were not many people about. The sky was high with hardly a cloud and they could hear the shrill shrieks from seagulls carried on the wind.

At the bottom of Folkungagatan they turned right and eventually reached the underpass to Fåfängan. Otto climbed up the wooden steps ahead of Elisabeth. She watched his sensible sports shoes and became acutely aware of her own sandals. Her feet looked wintry-white and she realised the transition from winter boots had happened without her noticing.

When they reached the peak of the hill Otto pointed to a bench.

'Let's sit here for a moment and catch our breath.'

The view was indeed magnificent. Directly below the steep cliff they could see the ferries operating the routes to Åland, Finland and the Baltic states, floating multi-storey buildings, almost small towns in themselves. To the left they had an unobstructed view over the Old Town with the Skeppsbron quay, from where the small white ferries hurried back and forth to Djurgården. Further away, the city sprawled in all directions.

Elisabeth sat with her eyes on the view, saying nothing.

'Beautiful, isn't it?'

She nodded.

'Have you lived in Stockholm long?' Otto asked.

She hesitated.

'In a way. And then in a way I haven't,' she said opaquely.

'I've lived here most of my life,' Otto said. 'But in a way I'm still an immigrant. I was five when I moved here with my mother from Austria. I have very few memories of living anywhere but here, yet those few memories seem more real, somehow more colourful, than any of the later ones.'

He paused briefly.

'Perhaps that's how it is with your earliest memories, whether or not you move?' he added.

When Elisabeth didn't respond, he continued.

'Most people have probably lived in more places than I have. Moved more often. My apartment here is only my fourth home. If it can be called that. I'm not sure that I've moved in properly, even though I have kept my things there and slept there for so many years. Lately I've begun to wonder if perhaps I've stayed too long in each place. Maybe I should have given more thought to where I really wanted to live.'

He closed his eyes and lifted his face to the sun.

Then he heard Elisabeth's voice.

'When I left Stockholm I was sure I would never come back. I was excited to leave it behind. My life here had not been particularly . . . happy. I was sure something else was waiting for me somewhere else. I didn't have any specific place in mind — I just wanted to get out of here. Begin again somewhere else. I felt

I was destined to live my real life far away from Stockholm.'

Otto opened his eyes and looked at her.

'And did you find that place?'

'I thought I did. For some time, I really did.'

She looked at him apprehensively, assessing whether to continue. Whether he could be trusted. He noted that her eyes were almost translucent in the bright light. Liquid honey with little dark specks. She turned away from him and returned her gaze to the view.

'For a long time I confused place with people. I thought I was in the right place because I thought I was with the right person.'

She gave him a quick serious look.

'If you can understand that.'

He nodded.

'And then, when I realised I no longer had that person, the place lost all meaning for me. I didn't know what to do. Where to go.'

There was a pause.

'So I came back. And now I think I understand that there was never anything wrong with this place. There was something wrong with me.' She pressed her clenched hand against her mouth, as if trying to hold back tears.

'How about a cup of coffee?' Otto said. 'Or perhaps some lunch? The shrimp sandwiches are good.'

She followed as Otto led the way to the restaurant.

THEY HAD FINISHED THEIR lunch and were sitting at a table in the garden outside the restaurant. The conversation had moved on to books and music. As usual, Otto was doing most of the talking.

'I did enjoy the book you gave me,' he said. 'I'm amazed you could read me so well.'

He gave her a quick look and smiled.

'You see, in many ways I used to be very like Mr Utz. As unhealthily attached to my books as he is to his Meissen porcelain. I suppose you could call it a kind of obsession. My entire life revolved around books. I read books at breakfast, I worked with books all day, and I read books in the evening. And when I was not reading books, I read *about* books. Reviews, articles. When I socialised, it was with other booky people.'

He was absently folding and unfolding a serviette as he spoke.

'When I was married, I never allowed myself to admit that I was unhappy. My wife and I never talked about how we felt. I have no idea whether she was happy or unhappy. It just was what it was. We lived together in a small house. We ate dinner together. We went on holidays together. I told myself that this was what married people did. This was what married life was all about. Or perhaps I didn't even do that — I have no memory of ever thinking about it consciously. We just attached another day to the ones before, and called it our life.'

He sighed deeply.

'When Eva died, well, perhaps I thought about it then. What our life together had been like. I think I allowed myself to acknowledge how unhappy I had been during our marriage. And I blamed her. Her coldness. The distance I always felt she kept.'

His eyes met Elisabeth's across the table.

'I must be boring you with my babble,' he said with an embarrassed shrug. 'I've never talked about this with anybody. I don't know what's come over me now.'

'You're not boring me, not at all. Shall I get us some more coffee?'

Otto nodded and Elisabeth left.

When she returned he looked up and smiled.

'Thank you,' he said as she placed his cup in front of him. He added sugar and sat stirring absent-mindedly.

'Did you have children?' Elisabeth asked as she sat down.

'No. No, we didn't. Things might have been different if we had; it's hard to know. But I don't think Eva was cut out for motherhood. She was fragile, petite. Very beautiful, at least I thought so. I used to think of her as an alabaster figurine. Exquisite. So white, so pure. Somehow it felt natural that her body would never carry a child. I never questioned it.'

He paused for a moment.

'It makes me think of Kaspar Utz again. And it makes me utterly sad.'

He leaned back against his chair and looked up.

'Do you have children, Elisabeth?'

She shook her head but made no comment.

'I'm not sure if I grieve over the children we never had. It's as hard for me to imagine myself as a father as it is for me to see Eva as a mother. I have no idea what kind of father I would have been.'

There was such sincere despair in his eyes that Elisabeth averted her own.

'Or what kind of husband I was. But I realise now that I was responsible for my actions. That I could have chosen to act differently. And this I mourn.'

'All those things we never did, the possibilities we never explored — we'll never know what might have been,' Elisabeth said. 'Nobody gets to experience every possibility. We have to make choices. And sometimes choices are made for us.'

Otto bent forward.

'But you see, Elisabeth, that's what bothers me most. That I assumed I knew what my wife wanted, when in effect it was just my own presumption. My ideas, my perceptions. And based on that, I made choices that affected us both. What kind of husband doesn't discuss the most important issues in life with his wife? Who believes he *knows*? Such terrible arrogance.'

His voice broke and he cleared his throat several times before he continued.

'In the book you gave me, Kaspar Utz makes a wiser choice than I managed to make. Before it was too late, he was able to choose life over his obsession. I have finally realised that I am able to give up mine. That I no longer need my books. But I'm afraid it's taken me too long to get to this point. I've allowed my whole life to slip by.'

Elisabeth leaned across the table and took Otto's hands in hers.

'Your life is not over yet, Otto. Every little insight is valuable. We don't need to think so very far ahead. Or have such detailed plans. Our lives keep unfolding one day at a time.'

Otto squeezed her hands and then he lifted one to his lips and gave it a kiss.

Elisabeth smiled before pulling her hand back.

'Perhaps we should make our way back?' Otto said. 'Shall we go along the water?'

21

I AM AN IDIOT, she thought. An absolute idiot. What am I doing?

Elisabeth stood by her kitchen window. Once again, she felt physically exhausted. Worse than after the first outing with Otto. But it was a comfortable kind of exhaustion. They had walked along the Hammarby canal, resting on a park bench halfway. They had not got home until after four. The intense sun had burnt her winter-pale face and her skin was hot.

I must be completely mad to have agreed to go, she reproached herself. How will I be able to decline next time?

She felt a lump in her throat. She filled a glass from the tap and drank it all in one go. It didn't help. Quite the opposite.

Sitting there dishing out words of wisdom about life. Me! It's grotesque.

She tore off her sandals and hurled them down the hall.

Ever since Otto had started shopping for her, she'd gradually become dependent on the fresh produce, and now she was hungry. That was it, exactly. All the needs and feelings that she had painfully pushed away were re-emerging. It was one thing to listen to Otto's stories over dinner. And to Elias's. Quite a different matter to spout on about her own. She simply could not allow it to continue. The road she had walked today inevitably led somewhere, and she knew she mustn't go there. With every day — every invitation, every favour she accepted — she was inexorably pulled closer to precisely what she had done everything to avoid.

This man with his kindness and his consideration, and today with his touching openness, had managed to penetrate the armour she had so painstakingly constructed around herself.

It was not comforting. It was painful.

She walked slowly towards the bedroom and from the doorway noticed that the bird had dropped to the floor. It upset her inexplicably and she hurried over to pick it up. She laid it carefully on the end of the bed, then she sat down next to it with her legs crossed. She gazed at the bird intently.

Why did this image have such an effect on her? She couldn't remember ever being moved in this way by a work of art. She ran the tips of her fingers over it, careful not to damage it.

'Why have you come to me, little bird? I'm not sure I want you here. I'm not sure I want any of this to happen to me. You, Otto, Elias — none of you. I want nothing. I don't want to need you. I don't want to need anything.'

She began to weep.

'Oh, for God's sake, not again. What is happening to me?'

She jumped up and went to the kitchen, returning with the roll of tape. She attached four strips to the wall and pressed the sheet of paper hard against the tape.

She stepped back.

'There. Yes, you stay there, little bird. You're nothing special to me; I just like you to sit there and watch me.'

She lay down on the bed, hands behind her head and her eyes on the bird.

'I don't know what you want with me, but I'll let you stay there for now. Until I know.'

THE WOMAN IN GREEN said nothing. Nothing at all. There was no need. Her expression was so very sad.

'Why do you come now?' Elisabeth whispered. 'I needed you before, but you were not here.'

'I am always with you.'

Elisabeth shook her head. 'No, you come and go.'

'That is because you make it so.'

'Are you saying I have power over you?' Elisabeth let out a short, incredulous laugh.

'You always had power over me.'

Elisabeth shook her head again. 'I never had any power over you. Or anything else in my life. I am completely powerless.'

'You are not. Not at all. I was always there for you. But only when you wanted me. And there were always many roads for you to choose from. I am only one.'

'I'm not choosing now.'

'You are always making choices, Elisabeth. I can't help you with your choices. I *am* one of them. And I can only be here when you choose me. When you understand that it is me you need.'

'Stay with me,' said Elisabeth.

The Woman in Green looked at her with her sad, dark eyes.

'I am always here when you want me.'

The doorbell rang.

'Wait!' Elisabeth cried as the Woman in Green faded. 'Please stay.'

But the image was lost and she was alone in the bedroom.

The doorbell rang again.

22

THERE HAD BEEN LITTLE time to talk to Elisabeth during the dinner at Otto's. And now that Maja had encouraged him, he had decided to ask Elisabeth to come and have another look at the drawings. He was not sure what he was hoping she might contribute, but it felt essential that he hear her thoughts.

He stood outside her door, waiting, unsure whether he should ring the doorbell a second time. He listened attentively but could hear no sound from the other side of the door. He pushed the button again, and finally she opened the door. She was fully dressed, but she looked as if she had just woken up.

'Sorry to bother you again,' Elias said, 'but we didn't get much chance at Otto's to talk about my project. Too much else to talk about, I guess! So I wanted to ask if you would mind coming over just to have a look. I couldn't help noticing that the pictures seemed to move you. That you saw something in them. It won't take long . . .'

'I'm not sure . . . I mean, what could I contribute?'

'It feels important to me to know what you think. And you must tell me honestly.'

Elisabeth ran her hand through her unkempt hair. She looked at him, her brow furrowed.

'Give me a minute or two and I'll come over,' she said eventually.

THERE WAS NO POINT trying to improve her appearance. He'd already seen the way things were with her: tousled hair, wrinkled clothes and no makeup. He must have known she had just got up. But she went to the bathroom and brushed her teeth. As she stood up after rinsing her mouth under the tap she met her own image in the mirror.

Here you go again, Elisabeth. You're even a little excited about it. Stupid, stupid woman. You can pretend as much as you like that you're just doing him a favour but you know it's not true. You want this for your own sake. Here you go again, even though you know it's hopeless and only extends the pain. Delays the inevitable. You can tell yourself it won't change anything but it will, Elisabeth. It will. All our actions affect matters. And not just for ourselves, of course. What we do affects everything.

She slowly ran a comb through her hair, all the while watching herself in the mirror. Why was it so hard for her to say no? Leave the door unopened? Shut her eyes and her ears to all stimuli? She had managed so well for so long. Now suddenly she had lost all control.

She took a bottle of perfume from the shelf and gave her throat and the insides of her wrists a quick spray.

You are a complete idiot, Elisabeth, she thought, leaning closer to the mirror. You're a fifty-three-year-old woman but you behave like a child. It's as if you're beginning to tell yourself there is something for you out there. As if you're beginning to hope. Let it go, Elisabeth. Let it go now.

She returned the perfume to the shelf and abruptly turned away from the mirror.

ELIAS OPENED THE DOOR the moment she put her finger on the button, as though he had been anxiously waiting just inside the door, worried that she might change her mind.

'Come in, Elisabeth,' he said. 'Thanks for coming. It means a lot to me.' He blushed and Elisabeth realised he was nervous. She couldn't understand why.

He walked ahead of her through the hallway.

'It's rather messy, I'm afraid,' he said over his shoulder. 'I haven't really been focused on anything other than this project since I came back.'

'Well, my place is always just so, as you know,' Elisabeth said.

Elias smiled. He stopped in the doorway to the living room.

'I have nothing much to offer you, but I do have a bottle of vodka in the freezer. Would you like a shot?'

'Oh . . . well, yes, why not?' Elisabeth heard herself saying.

Elias stepped aside to allow her to enter the living room while he went to the kitchen to get the drinks.

When he returned, he found her standing bent over the drawings on the floor. She accepted the misty glass of vodka without taking her eyes off them. She took a small sip but said nothing. Elias sat down on his work chair by the table, nervously fingering his glass. Then he emptied it in one gulp, placed the glass on the table and fired up his laptop to play some music. As the first notes sounded, Elisabeth turned to face him.

'That's the music Otto played, isn't it?' she said.

'Yes. It's Rachmaninov's Piano Trio No. 1. It's one of Otto's favourite pieces. He's been trying to teach me a bit about music. It's like for the first time in my life I'm actually learning things. I didn't have a great time at school. Well, you know about my reading. And without that, nothing else made sense. It was a shit of a time. But with Otto teaching me it's completely different. Books, music, geography, biology . . . He seems to know so much and I am learning without even being aware of it.'

All of a sudden, he jumped up. 'Sorry, here I am sitting on the only chair. So sorry . . . here, you sit down.'

But Elisabeth remained standing, lost in thought.

'Can I see the smaller drawings too?' she asked eventually.

'Of course!' Elias picked up the drawing pads from the table.

'Sorry I don't have a sofa. Or a coffee table. Do you mind if we sit on the floor? That's what I usually do. Or lie down on my bed.'

He blushed and Elisabeth laughed. It was so unexpected that it was a moment before Elias joined in.

They sat side by side with their backs to the wall and the drawing pads in front of them. Elisabeth turned the pages slowly, sometimes going back a page before lifting the next leaf. All the time she was quiet. No questions, no comments.

When she had finally gone right through both the pads she looked up. Elias thought she looked very pale and her brown eyes seemed both larger and darker.

'Such a sad story,' she said at last. 'So very sad.'

'But it's not finished,' Elias said quietly. 'I haven't got to the end yet.'

Elisabeth sat looking straight ahead of her.

'It's also very beautiful . . . much more beautiful than reality,' she said.

Elias scrambled to his feet and disappeared from the room, returning with the vodka bottle in hand. He looked questioningly at Elisabeth and she nodded. He filled both glasses and handed her one.

'What did you mean when you said it was more beautiful than reality?'

She thought for a while.

'They are such beautiful images, Elias. Even the horrendous is somehow beautiful. The sorrow, the desperation — you have given them a heartbroken beauty. In real life they are not beautiful. Just brutal and ugly. But in your world they are both. Horrendous, and very beautiful.'

Suddenly she covered her face with her hands.

Elias sat with his glass in his hand, unsure what to do.

She lowered her hands and looked at him.

'I don't know, Elias. Perhaps there is a kind of beauty in the desperation of real life, but not for the people involved. There might be a kind of beauty in tragedy, when looked at from the outside. But from the inside, it's ugly.'

Now she was weeping, but it was a quiet weeping, soundless. Tears streamed down her cheeks.

'I am frightened by your pictures,' she said.

'Frightened by them?'

'I am. Because I know the story your pictures are telling, and I don't want to hear it. But I can't tear my eyes away. And I'll never be able to forget them.'

'Vodka?' Elias asked, holding up the bottle.

'I'm not sure how this will end,' she said with a weak smile. She raised her glass and toasted him.

'Can you write, Elisabeth?'

'Write?'

'Yes. Have you ever written anything?'

She didn't reply.

'I don't know anything about you, really. What kind of job you have or anything.'

She didn't return his gaze, but emptied her glass and placed it on the floor.

'Shall I tell you a little about me?' Elias said. 'About my drawings and my work?'

She said nothing.

'I really have only one talent. I'm good at only one thing. I can draw. That's all. So for me it was never a choice. I have drawn and painted all my life. At the start my mother encouraged me, but that changed. I suppose she wanted what was best for me, in her way. As long as I was a child my art was all right, but she wanted me to grow up. Get myself a proper job. Earn a living. By then I already knew it had to be this.'

He filled both their glasses again, this time without asking.

'Anyway, eventually my pictures became stories. Later, when I had studied art and came to realise I would never become a great artist, I returned to my stories. My cartoon stories.'

He leaned back and closed his eyes for a moment, before continuing.

'I have a best friend, Maja. We're . . . well, Maja and I have

133

always known each other. Maja writes, I draw. That's how it's always been since we were little. But then it turned into a real job. Something we could make a living from. So when I started this project I assumed we would work on it together as usual. But Maja can't do this one. She doesn't have the time, but also, when she saw the drawings she said she was not the right person to write this. That it was too difficult.'

Elias rose and walked to the window. He opened it and stood looking out, his back to Elisabeth.

'I'm not sure what it is with this story. It's somehow . . . well, different.'

He turned and looked at her. The room was very still and the sounds from outside drifted in through the window.

'I'm not sure how to say this . . .'

He looked so uncomfortable that Elisabeth felt she had to say something.

'You can tell me anything, Elias. Don't worry.'

'It was after I had left that envelope for you. I just couldn't stop thinking about you. About the person inside your apartment. I noticed you the day you moved in but I'd not seen you at all after that. So I began to form my own picture of you.'

He turned back to the window.

'I began to make sketches — that's how I always start. I never know at that stage what kind of story it will turn into. I have no idea why this figure became a bird, but as soon as I saw it, it felt right, somehow.'

He turned back to look at her.

'I'm sure you think this sounds weird. But I'm somehow also hoping you will understand.'

Elisabeth slowly got up.

She stood in front of him and gently placed her hand on his arm. Then she shook her head.

'No, Elias, I don't think it's weird. And I do believe I understand. It moves me so that you somehow managed to reach through that closed door. That you didn't just leave.'

Elias sat down on the floor again and Elisabeth sat close beside him. She looked at him, but he didn't acknowledge her gaze. He sat with his hands clasped around his knees.

She realised he was struggling to get the words out. All she could do was to wait. Give him the time he needed.

Finally, he looked up.

'So, I wonder, Elisabeth, could you do it? Would you write the words for my story? Because, really, it's your story.'

23

THE DREAMS LINGERED LIKE morning mist, and dissolved as she emerged from sleep. Reluctantly she opened her eyes and, as she did, the remnants of the dreams slipped away. They had been strange, unusual dreams, and they had left her with an odd sense of . . . She was not sure how to describe it. Hope? No. Relief? A weight had not exactly come off her shoulders, but shifted. Something inside her had been relieved a little, for now at least.

She closed her eyes again. Her mouth felt dry and she needed to pee. But she wanted to stay inside dream mode a bit longer. Somehow, it felt as if the dream were a continuation of the evening before.

She had been drunk, no doubt about that. But she regretted nothing of what had been said or done. And she remembered every word, every nuance of the conversation.

Her first instinct had been to get up, say goodnight and leave. Escape into the safety of her darkness. But before she managed to rise from the floor he stood in front of her with his hand on her shoulder.

'I'm sorry if I'm bothering you. I don't mean to intrude on your private life.'

'No, no. That's not it. I just think I've had too much to drink and I should leave now.'

He kneeled in front of her and grabbed both her arms.

'Maja told me that what we really need often comes to us. That we just have to be observant, make sure not to miss the smallest signs. When I watched you looking at my drawings I thought I saw the sign. I know you understand them — you can hear my story. Our story.'

His gaze was intense and he kept hold of her arms. She looked into his grey eyes, so open she felt she could see straight into him. And momentarily she was plunged back into the sense of helplessness she had felt when she bent down over his bleeding body on the pavement. A need to protect something pure and innocent.

Finally she had to look away.

'You see, Elisabeth, the only person I've ever met who has understood my drawings and the stories they tell is Maja. And she said these ones were beyond her ability. But you understand them, don't you? You can hear my story?'

There was a new intensity in his voice. As if her response meant everything.

Finally, she had looked up.

'Yes,' she said quietly. 'I think I do hear the story.'

He let go of her arms and sat back on his heels.

'So would you write it for me?'

She stared at him. Then she slowly shook her head and looked away. When finally she looked at him again she saw that he was sitting with his head tilted towards the ceiling and his eyes closed. He was weeping.

He moved back beside her with his legs pulled up in front of him. He said nothing.

'Listen to me, Elias,' she said, and now it was she who kneeled in front of him. She bent forward and placed her hand on his cheek. 'Listen.'

He made no sign of having heard her.

'I *can* hear your story, but I can't write it. I just can't. I have . . . Well, it's just not possible. I'm so very sorry.' Now she was weeping, too.

She sat back down beside him.

'Your story deserves the most beautiful, expressive words; the most poetic text imaginable. I just can't write like that. I can't write at all. I am not your sign.'

She slid her hand behind his neck.

'Elias, look at me.'

He pulled away.

'Look at me. Listen to me.'

He opened his eyes and turned his face to her.

'I live in there, inside my darkness, because that's all I can do. I have nothing at all to give. I'm just trying to get through one day at a time. What I once had, I have lost, and there's no way I can have it back. It's been destroyed, once and for all. I have lost absolutely everything. I don't mean belongings, nothing like that. I mean all that makes life meaningful. My very self. And when you have lost that, well, you're no longer alive, really. Even if your heart beats and your lungs inhale oxygen. It's strange how your body can continue to function when it no longer fulfils a purpose. It shouldn't be possible.'

She fell silent.

'I shouldn't be here. I should never have opened that damned door.' Her voice broke. 'But here I am, and I am so sorry.'

Elias still said nothing.

Eventually Elisabeth cleared her throat and continued.

'But you, Elias — you have an exceptional talent. Don't ever allow anybody to convince you otherwise. Just like you protected your hands, you have to protect everything that makes you who you are, and never let anybody take it from you.'

He looked thoughtful, took her hand and lifted it to his cheek.

'Absolutely everything that you are is worth protecting and sheltering, Elias. And celebrating. Remember to be who you are, and understand that only those who love the person you really are, really love you. Look at yourself, Elias!'

He shook his head as she rose.

For a moment she stood looking down at him, as if unsure of

what to do next. Then she drew a deep breath.

'Come,' she said, and took his hands. 'Come here with me.'

He scrambled reluctantly to his feet and she pulled him with her to the mirror in the hallway.

'Stand here,' she said, and pointed to the floor in front of the mirror. 'Now look at yourself, and tell me what you see.'

Elias stood in front of the mirror, stiff and self-conscious.

'Tell me something. Hair colour?'

'Brown, I guess.'

'Chestnut. Thick and very beautiful. Eyes?'

'Grey.'

She shook her head. 'Step closer to the mirror.'

'Well, mixed, then. A little green and a little grey.'

She nodded. 'With thick dark curly eyelashes. They are beautiful, Elias. Can't you see that?' She smiled and moved to stand closely behind him.

'Take off your shirt.'

He looked surprised.

'Just do it.'

He slowly pulled off his t-shirt and dropped it to the floor.

'Describe what you see.'

'Well, a pale upper body . . .'

'A wide-shouldered, really attractive torso, I would say. Strong arms.' She lifted his right arm. 'And a hand that can create drawings that make people weep.'

He laughed. 'You're crazy . . .'

'Yes, I told you, didn't I? Now remove your jeans.'

'No, that's enough, Elisabeth.'

She shook her head.

'Take them off.'

He unbuttoned his jeans and slowly stepped out of them.

'And your underwear. I'll close my eyes if you like. This is not for me, it's for you.'

She closed her eyes and heard him remove his underwear.

'Now I'm opening my eyes,' she said. She stood close behind him and placed her hands very lightly on his back.

'Can you see it now, Elias? Can you see how beautiful you are?'

He stood absolutely still, arms at his sides and looking straight into the mirror.

Then he turned around and embraced her, lifting her from the floor.

When he finally put her down he stood calmly before her. She smiled and stroked his chest.

'Remember this, Elias. Always. Not how you *look*, but how it *feels*. You are all of this. Your thoughts, your ideas, your talent, your body — together they make up the whole that is you. Don't ever allow the parts to be separated. Never accept being loved partially, because that's not love. Someone who loves you, loves all of you. All of you just as you are.'

She smiled and placed her hands on his shoulders.

'And now it's definitely time for me to go home.'

'Wait,' Elias said, and started to pull on his jeans. Elisabeth stretched out a supporting hand when he wobbled.

'Come here.'

He dragged her back into the living room.

'Sit down,' he said, and she reluctantly obeyed. Elias walked to the desk and put on some more music.

'This is new to me,' she said.

He sat down beside her. 'Otto only listens to piano trios since we met you. This is Mendelssohn's Piano Trio No. 1, the second movement.'

They sat side by side on the floor, listening. When the music finished Elias went and fetched something from his desk. He returned to Elisabeth and held out a USB memory stick.

'This is *The Blackbird*,' he said. 'All the pictures. I had prepared them for you, hoping you would agree to be my writer. But I want you to have them anyway.'

She stretched up and kissed him on the cheek.

'You will find your writer. I know you will,' she said.

———

ELISABETH GOT UP AND went to the bathroom. After she had showered she stood by the open window in the living room holding a mug of tea. Her head was heavy and her mouth felt dry, yet she was filled with a sense of warmth she could not quite explain. The sun shone over the small playground across the street but there were no children around. She was not sure, but it might be a holiday. There were so many holidays at this time of year.

She turned back to her books and picked up the pile of unsorted papers. The one she had thrown across the floor in frustration. Afterwards she had just gathered the sheets together and dropped the pile on the floor.

She took it into the kitchen, sat down at the table and started to sort the numbered pages into order. Then she went to the bedroom, where she ran her hand along the top shelf of the wardrobe until she felt the laptop and charging cable. Back in the kitchen, she placed the computer on the bench and plugged in the charger. She wasn't sure it would still take the charge — she couldn't remember when she had last used it.

It took her all afternoon to read the manuscript. Every so often she had to take a break. Stand up and walk a few laps around the apartment. Splash cold water on her face. Have a drink. But she didn't cry.

It was early evening when she turned the last page. She placed her hand on top of the pile.

Why had she kept it? And why had she brought it here? It was like carrying a dead body. A corpse. Worse, it was the body of something that had never lived.

24

IT WAS WHITSUN EVE and the whole city was in bloom. Otto stood by his open kitchen window, looking out. Although he could only see the façade of the building across the courtyard and the tops of the trees below, he could sense how empty the city was. And he remembered how it felt when he was a child. As if he and his mother were the only two people left in the city. These days it usually didn't concern him in the least; rather the opposite. Usually he felt a sense of relief when the city became his own. But right now, right here, he felt strangely affected by the thought of the vacated city outside. A little melancholy.

He had extended his walks further and further during the past week. One day he caught the ferry across to Djurgården and spent all day there, including lunch at Blå Porten. He couldn't remember when he'd last been there. While Eva was still alive they used to visit the spring salon at Liljewalchs Konsthall. Eva was interested in art and she painted. Some of her watercolours still hung in his apartment. Pale, dreamlike landscapes. Not bad, but not good enough to be exhibited or sold.

After Eva's death his visits to galleries and museums had grown more and more infrequent, until eventually they stopped entirely. He realised he missed them in a way. More than the visits as such, he missed the companionship of doing something with another human being. That sense of sharing impressions, laughing and crying at the same things. It was never like that with Eva. Even though they had wandered through the same exhibitions and walked the same walks, he had never really felt they shared the experience. Thinking about it now, he wondered if he had ever experienced real companionship since he was a young child.

Why had he not made more effort in all these years since she died? Apart from the friendship with Elias, his life was almost entirely lacking in social contact. He had a couple of old friends he still kept in touch with, and whom he met a couple of times a year. One was Åke, who owned a summer place at Ekholmen. Åke was a bachelor — as far as Otto knew he had never been married, and he had no children. Their friendship — if you could call it that; perhaps they were more like acquaintances? — was not the kind where you shared personal matters.

Åke had been employed in Otto's bookshop for many years, and when Eva died he had invited Otto to his summer place. Eventually it developed into an annual tradition: Otto would visit Ekholmen for a couple of weeks every summer. They usually overlapped for one week, then Otto had the place to himself for a week. He liked it, especially the second week. He smiled to himself thinking about it. The fact that it was the week alone he enjoyed the most. Had he become too accustomed to being by himself?

He'd never had a country place of his own. Unlike most born and bred Swedes he had no base in another part of the country, or relatives in the countryside. In fact any relatives at all. He had never really considered himself a particularly sociable person, but he remembered how his mother had made friends in different ways. Work colleagues, neighbours, people she met in a variety of contexts. She seemed to have a large circle of friends. But he wondered if she had missed having a man in her life. She'd been a young woman when his father died — just a little over forty, with more than half her life ahead of her. She died in her eighty-sixth year. Had her friends and acquaintances fulfilled her need for close relationships? What about her only son? Otto didn't remember her as physically affectionate, but as infinitely considerate, loyal and encouraging in every way. As an adult he had probably considered her his best friend. It had been just the two of them for so long.

EVERY TIME OTTO PASSED Elisabeth's door on his way out he was tempted to ring her doorbell. But he refrained, thinking she probably wanted to be left alone. Perhaps she would take the initiative when she was ready? But days had passed since their visit to Fåfängan and he'd not seen or heard her. Elias had come for dinner as usual the Tuesday after their little party, but neither of them had suggested that they should invite Elisabeth. Elias seemed a bit preoccupied and Otto put it down to his project. In fact he had excused himself early to get back to it. As they stood in the hallway saying goodbye, it struck Otto that Elias exuded a newfound confidence. He held his head a little higher, his shoulders a little further back. Working on *The Blackbird* must be good for him, Otto had thought.

Now here Otto was, in front of his open window. It was early evening and the blackbird's song echoed between the stone walls in the courtyard. The lilacs had opened and the fragrance drifted inside in delicate breaths. It was almost six. And he was alone.

IT TOOK HIM JUST twenty minutes to tidy up in the kitchen, put a bottle of champagne in the freezer for a quick chill, and have a shower and shave.

He stood with his hair still wet and a little out of breath, his finger hovering uncertainly over the doorbell. He pressed it. Nothing happened. He'd decided that if she didn't open on the first ring, he'd leave her alone. He stuck his hands in his pockets and rocked from his toes to his heels and back again. No sound. He threw a quick glance at Elias's door, but he knew he was out with Maja and her friends. In fact, it felt as if the whole house were empty and he was completely alone where he stood.

He heard the soft steps and she opened the door.

'I thought it might be you,' she said.

'I just wanted to ask if you felt like a little supper. I wasn't sure you'd be here — everybody seems to be away for the weekend.'

'Come in,' she said. 'I've actually made a bit of an effort in here. Unpacked a little. Even cleaned.'

He stepped inside and she closed the door, gesturing for him to go into the living room.

Tidy it might have been, but for some reason it looked even more desolate than before. Previously, it had been possible to imagine that when it was all unpacked and arranged it would feel like a home. But this was the saddest home Otto had ever seen. In the living room the books lay in piles along one wall, with the flattened removal boxes folded and piled up in front of them. There was not one piece of furniture in the room. The floor was clean, as was the slightly open window. But it was a desert of a room.

'Well,' she said, and let her arm fall to her side, 'not much of an improvement, is it?'

He shrugged. 'It will come, it will come.'

She looked at him for a moment, then gazed around the room.

'Do you really think so?'

'Absolutely. All good things take time.'

'I'm not so sure. It seems to me that good things happen in a flash, but bad things take time. And they last.'

She paused.

'I have my doubts about this place. I really do. I'm not sure it's possible for me to live here.'

She turned and stood facing him.

'I have nothing to offer you.'

Otto made a dismissive gesture.

'But that's why I'm here. I've already prepared a very simple little supper of sorts upstairs, at my place. It would make me very happy if you would share it with me.'

Her eyes seemed enormous in her pinched, pale face.

'Wait for me in the kitchen,' she said, and disappeared into the bedroom.

He noticed a thick pile of what looked like unopened mail on the kitchen table. But there were no ornaments of any kind, and no tablecloth. A small table lamp on the windowsill. The empty bench was wiped clean — not a dish in sight. At one end of the counter sat a laptop, and on top of it a black notebook with a rubber band around it. It surprised him a little, for some reason. Perhaps because it was a sign of life in this apparently uninhabited space. He was relieved when he heard her steps in the hall.

She was about to close the door behind them when she stopped.

'I forgot something. I won't be a moment.' She disappeared briefly, then they set off upstairs.

―――――

OTTO HAD PREPARED A large bowl of unpeeled shrimp, mayonnaise, a basket of toast and a small cheese board with three kinds of cheese, fresh figs and walnuts. On the bench there was a glass bowl with strawberries, and the table was set for two. He cast a quick glance over it all and realised what a sad figure he would have made sitting there by himself.

'Please, have a seat,' he said, pulling out a chair. 'Simple, as you can see. I was planning on a solitary evening — I didn't want to intrude on you again — but then . . . well, I decided to be brave and ask you, although it was short notice. Hoping you wouldn't take offence.'

'Why should I take offence?'

'Well, you never know. I have been rather pushy . . .'

She smiled and shook her head.

'I would have said no if I had not wanted to come. Or simply not opened the door. As is my habit.' She smiled.

All that could be heard when Otto opened the champagne was a soft sigh.

'No mark on the ceiling this time. A shame, really — I should have let the cork pop properly. Add another memory of a special evening.'

He handed her a glass and poured.

'I hope it's cold enough,' he said.

Otto held out his glass to make a toast. Elisabeth raised hers, too.

'Skål! Cheers to . . .' Otto searched for the right word.

'To friendship?' Elisabeth said.

'To hope?' he added.

Elisabeth turned her glass in her hand.

'Oh, but hope requires that you can imagine tomorrow. For me, here and now is enough.'

He was just about to speak when the blackbird in the courtyard below began to sing again. They listened for a moment in silence.

'It's easy to think it sings only for us, isn't it?' Otto said finally. 'A solace for those left in the city.'

'I think it does,' said Elisabeth. The blackbird sings for us only. Tonight.'

———

THE EARLY JUNE EVENING had settled over the city, a kind of exhalation after the day. A tiny adjustment of light and temperature, nothing more.

And the blackbird was singing.

Elisabeth and Otto were still at the kitchen table. Otto had poured white wine and brought the strawberries and the cheese to the table.

'You're not asking me anything,' Elisabeth said suddenly.

Otto looked up, surprised.

'Should I be?'

'Surely, you must have wondered . . .'

'Not really. Elias was curious about you at the start, and I suppose I began to wonder who you were. Since we never saw you come out of your apartment. But Elias's wondering led to something tangible — he began to draw.'

Elisabeth smiled as she hulled a strawberry.

'It was a bit strange that we never saw you, but no. The answer to your question is no. I didn't really wonder. I gave you no thought at all. We have other neighbours that I don't know and rarely see. And I certainly don't wonder what their lives are like.'

Elisabeth looked at him and the flames of the candles on the table were reflected in her eyes. For the first time he allowed himself to consciously acknowledge that she was beautiful. So beautiful that he was afraid his thoughts would be revealed in his gaze, his gestures, his words.

'But that's all changed, of course. Now that I know who you are.'

Elisabeth smiled a little.

'Now that you know what it looks like inside my apartment. How I live. I would have expected that to lead to questions, but I'm relieved it hasn't.'

'Perhaps that's my real problem,' said Otto. 'I wonder too little; don't care enough. I don't really think about anything other than what I see and sense directly. I view people with less interest and compassion than I regard my books.'

'Is that so bad? I'm sure it can be liberating. For both parties. It's not really very meaningful to engage with people you don't know. Or haven't even seen.'

'Hmm. I think that depends. You dashed out to help Elias even though you didn't know him.'

'That was different. Helping a person in distress — it's like helping an animal. Anybody. It requires no commitment. You just do it instinctively.'

'Sure, it requires commitment! Lots of it! Think of all those people who indifferently step over injured and dying people without lifting a finger. Or caring at all.'

'It's still not the same as being genuinely interested in another human being.'

Otto went to the fridge and took out another bottle of wine.

'This will be our third bottle, Otto,' Elisabeth said, shaking her head. 'God knows how this will end.'

'Yes, I know. But it's Whitsun Eve. And we're all alone. You and me and the blackbird.'

He sat down and filled their glasses.

'To return to my initial question: I did notice the look on your face when you stepped inside my place earlier. I know how it looks. I have no furniture, no art. I've unpacked my books but I don't even have a bookcase. Mopping the floors and cleaning the windows made it worse, if anything. I can see that. Before, it was possible to look at it and assume that there would be furniture arriving. New curtains and rugs. That it was just a matter of time . . .'

She looked at him with a thoughtful expression.

'But I don't know if I will ever move in properly. Or move out.'

'There is no rush, Elisabeth. Look at me! I am almost sixty-nine and I'm still living in temporary accommodation. When I moved here I would not have been able to envisage myself living here fifteen years later. I dumped my things, and as they landed then, they are still standing today.'

She shook her head.

'It's not the same. You see, I don't know if I want to live anywhere at all.'

The kitchen became very still. And it was silent outside, too. As if everything was holding its breath.

Otto stood up and walked around the table. He took Elisabeth's hands and gently pulled her to her feet. Then he put his arms around her and held her gently.

'Hush,' he whispered. 'I am so happy that you are here, in the same building as me. There is no need to think beyond this moment. For either of us.'

They stood absolutely still in the semi-dark kitchen.

'Tell you what, Elisabeth. I think we should go down and sit in the courtyard. The garden furniture is back outside. Let's take our wine and the strawberries.'

She didn't move, and he gently stroked her hair.

'What do you say?'

She slowly released herself from his arms and took a step back, dried her eyes with her hands and smiled thinly.

'I think it sounds like a brilliant idea, that's what I say.'

MUCH LATER THEY WERE still in the courtyard. Otto had collected a blanket for Elisabeth and a jersey for himself. They sat close together on the wooden bench and Otto had his arm around Elisabeth's shoulders.

'We toasted to hope before,' he said. 'What I really had in mind was a toast to love. But I have begun to wonder if I have not led a life without love. Perhaps that's why I proposed a toast to hope instead. When I think about it, hope might be more important. The hope of love. When you no longer have hope, then surely it is impossible to love. Or accept love.'

He paused.

'I do think my mother loved me, but she had so many sorrows to bear that they often seemed to take over. Her grief over what she had lost overshadowed the joy over what she still had. I think that often happens. Somehow, grief seems to take up more space than happiness. But in her way, my mother did love me, of that I am quite sure. And I loved her.

'I lived at home for so long — I stayed on at university working on a PhD. My world was very small: I had very few friends. My mother told me I was too serious, that I always had my nose in some book when I ought to be going out and having fun. But I didn't really know how to do that. Then I met the man who came to decide my choice of occupation, Axel Borgström his name was. I met him by chance at the Royal Library where I spent a lot of my time. We discovered that we shared many interests and he invited me to visit his bookshop: the one that eventually became mine.

I dropped my research and started to work for him. Well, and then I met Eva. So you see I have had a rather uneventful life.'

'In what way?'

'Not much love, I suppose. One relationship only, one marriage. There might have been the odd brief relationship before I met Eva, but I wouldn't have called them love. And now I have begun to question my marriage, too. And . . . well, then there is nothing left at all.'

'But love isn't just about relationships, is it? I have started to think it is more like an ability. Something you are capable of. Or not. And which can express itself in many different ways. But more than anything, I think that much of what we call love is something altogether different. Sometimes, it is the opposite.'

'Yes, it's not always that easy to know. I thought I fell in love when I met Eva, but what did I know about love? Did I love Eva? Now, I honestly don't know. I obviously thought I did.'

Elisabeth seemed to shiver.

'Are you cold?'

She shook her head, but he still pulled her closer to him.

'They say that if you *think* you might be having a heart attack, it rarely is one. That you *know* if it really is one. Perhaps that's how it is with love. If you're not certain, then it isn't really love. But if you've never experienced it before, how can you be sure? Sadly, it seems that you can only know in hindsight. When you have something to compare it to. Also, and saddest of all, is the fact that so many of us seem to resign ourselves to what we have. That we stick the label *love* on almost anything. And extinguish our hope for the real thing.'

They sat in stillness. All the windows on the façade were black except for Otto's kitchen window, which was glowing warmly yellow. 'We make ourselves believe that love will come to us, that it will satisfy all our needs, fulfil all our hopes and dreams, and that it will last forever. We believe that we love, when in reality we want to *be* loved,' Elisabeth said quietly. 'We project our feelings on one human being, and instantly we lose sight of all the others surrounding us. Those who might be capable of giving us love. Maybe we can never get all the love we crave from one person. But

154

small gifts of love taken together can make up more than anything we can expect from one individual.'

'On the other hand, Elisabeth, when you say that being able to love is a capacity, then I wonder if it isn't also a capacity to be able to accept love. Allow yourself to be loved. I think that this ability is at least as important. But perhaps this is what you mean?'

Elisabeth gave a short laugh.

'I'm not sure what I mean any more. I'm not going to try to untangle my thoughts tonight. I'm just going to sit here for a moment longer and not think at all.' But she looked at him with a thoughtful expression, as if unable to let go entirely of what he had said. The morning was subtly making itself felt. The sky above them was no longer as intensely dark blue.

And at that moment the blackbird started to sing again.

Otto bent over Elisabeth and gave the top of her head a kiss.

She looked up at him, placed her hands on his cheeks and kissed him on the mouth.

Then she stood, and from the pocket of her jeans she pulled a key, which she held out to him.

'Can you please keep this for me? Just in case.'

She took his hand, turned the palm upwards and placed the key on it, closing his fingers around it.

25

THE SUN WAS NOT yet visible above the horizon but the sky was illuminated and to the east the blue was turning into a pink mist.

Elias walked slowly across the churchyard. He gazed over the small new graves, all decorated with plants and cut flowers. There was a remarkable sharpness to it all. The colours seemed translucent; the fragrances embraced him. He stopped and sat down on one of the park benches.

The party had been the same as every year, just as Maja had predicted. The same venue — Maja's mother's little allotment cottage at Tanto, the same people and the same food. Even the same music. It had turned into an annual tradition and it had gradually become a point not to change anything from year to year. But the weather had been unusually nice. Elias remembered wet and rainy parties. This year it had been perfect. And Maja had brought a new guest, Paul, a French photographer. She had introduced him to Elias and then gone back to whatever she was doing in the miniature kitchen. Paul and Elias had stood on the lawn surrounded by the just-opened lilacs, sipping their beers. Paul had been smoking and Elias had filled his lungs with the cool scented air. They talked in English; Elias's French was virtually non-existent. Paul was in Sweden on a brief visit to take photos for an article about Stieg Larsson's Stockholm for a French literary magazine.

When Maja had introduced them she had put one arm around Elias's shoulders and the other around Paul's.

'Paul,' she said, 'this is my very best friend. His name is Elias Blom and he is Sweden's — perhaps the world's — best cartoonist. And this, Elias, is a very new friend of mine, Paul Pascinsky. He is France's — if not the world's — best photographer. And we call him Pepe. I have a feeling you two will like each other.'

She had laughed and disappeared again. Elias had felt his cheeks blush, but like Paul he joined in the laughter. He realised he had not laughed like this for such a very long time. He searched desperately for something to say, but Paul beat him to it.

'So, you're a cartoon artist?' he said, cocking his head and exhaling smoke through the corner of his mouth.

Elias managed a nod.

'You Swedes are so good at that, so if it's true what Maja says, that you are one of the best, you must be very, very good.'

'Oh, I don't know,' Elias said, hoping his cheeks were not as obviously red in the slight dusk as they felt to him. 'I can't tell if I'm any good at it. But I know I couldn't do it without Maja. I'm only good with images, not words.'

'Same!' Paul smiled.

Paul asked Elias about his books and was very impressed when he heard that three of them had been published in France.

Just then Maja called for them to take their seats at the dining table. As usual at Maja's parties, the conversation spanned a variety of topical issues, with swells of passionate discussion. Paul seemed very comfortable in the new company, and contributed as much as anybody to the conversation. After dinner they spread out over the small veranda, on the stone steps that led down into the garden and on blankets on the grass. The dew began to set over the garden and the grass was damp but it was not cold, and it was too early in the season for mosquitos.

Elias and Paul ended up on the steps, Paul one below Elias.

After a little while Paul leaned back against Elias's shins. Elias sat absolutely still as the warmth from Paul's back penetrated his jeans and then his skin.

Paul and Elias stayed and helped Maja tidy up and lock the cottage, then they walked together to the Southern Station. Outside the station building they said goodbye and Elias gave Maja a hug. As he stretched out his hand to say goodbye to Paul, Paul grabbed it in a firm grip and pulled him close, giving him a peck on the cheek. Elias noticed how Maja smiled smugly, but she said nothing.

'I would really like to see you again,' Paul said. 'Perhaps we can have lunch one day? I am here for another five days.'

'I would love that,' Elias said, and pulled out his wallet. 'Here is my card. Give me a ring.'

ELIAS LOOKED OUT OVER the abandoned churchyard. He had never seen it like this. So clearly that every blade of grass, every petal stood out. Yes, he had had a smoke or two, and during the course of the evening he had had quite a few beers. But he was not under the influence now.

He was happy.

The house was silent when he walked up the few steps to the front door. Hanging on his door handle was a plastic bag. Intrigued, he unhooked it and took a look inside. Papers — the whole bag was full of papers. He unlocked the door and went inside, kicked off his shoes and walked barefoot into the living room. There was no need to turn on the light: it was already daylight outside. He placed the heavy bag on the table and slid out the contents. The thick pile of papers was tied with a narrow green ribbon. On top there was a folded note:

Dear Elias,
I know how difficult it is for you to read, so you might rightly wonder

why I am giving you this. There is no need to read any further, but I think Otto would be happy to help you if that is what you want. I'm leaving this in your hands now. I don't want it back. You are free to do with it what you want.

He read only these first lines, then he folded the note again and placed it on the table. He untied the green ribbon and lifted the cover sheet. It was tattered, as if it had been handled carelessly. On it there were just two words:

Broken Wings

He thought it sounded vaguely familiar, but then it was not a particularly original title. He looked again at the pile. There was no way he could read it all. He tidied the edges of the papers, placed the note on top and re-tied the green ribbon around it.

He crossed the floor to the window. The sun hadn't quite reached the rooftops but the sky was gossamer pale blue, without a cloud.

26

THE WEATHER TURNED AND it became chilly again. It seemed as if the progress of summer had come to a standstill and the city had reverted to its introverted state after a couple of weeks of unashamed exaltation.

Otto sat at the kitchen table with a cup of tea. He had closed the window that had been left open overnight but the kitchen still felt cold. Open in front of him on the table was the first book Elisabeth had given him, *A Book of Common Prayer*. He had placed his hand on the open page, but his unseeing eyes were fixed on the window.

I don't think that I have ever known anybody who has lived such an unexamined life.

He couldn't get the sentence out of his head. How was it to be interpreted? Was it one's own self-examination that the author was referring to? Or a lack of interest in one's surroundings? His own life was certainly unexamined — by himself as well as by others. In fact, it was unlikely that anybody other than his handful of family and friends had ever even given a thought to his life. Nor had he himself. It was only now that he was retrieving his memories and making an attempt at interpreting them. He had thought a lot about Eva, and he realised now with terrible clarity that her life, too, seemed entirely unexamined. Because he had shown so little interest himself in her life, he couldn't be sure how much consideration she herself might have given it. It was impossible to know even if she had been happy or unhappy. She had rarely talked about her childhood or early life, and he had not been particularly keen to find out. No wonder their marriage had been so . . . so pitifully undeveloped.

He closed the book with a sigh and was just about to get up when the doorbell rang. He was not expecting anyone and he couldn't imagine who it might be.

'Elisabeth!' he said with genuine surprise as he opened the door. 'Come in!'

She stepped inside hesitantly.

'Can I offer you anything? A cup of coffee?'

She shook her head.

'I'm just wondering if you are planning to go to the supermarket.'

'Oh, well, I haven't really thought about it yet. But sure, yes, I do most days. Just to get some air. As an excuse to take me outside.'

She looked at him for a moment.

'Can I come?'

For a brief moment Otto was speechless, but he collected himself quickly.

'Of course! When do you want to go?'

'Oh, anytime, really. I'll fit in with your plans. I suppose I could go by myself, but I feel a little . . . Well, I haven't been out much, and I'm still a little lost. It would be good to have company.'

'I'll come down in half an hour. Will that suit?'

She nodded, took a step forward and kissed him lightly on the cheek.

'Thank you for the other night. A magical evening.'

And she turned abruptly and left.

HE SAW THAT HER door was ajar when he came downstairs and Elisabeth appeared as soon as he reached the landing. She seemed to have dressed with a little more care than usual — the same pair of jeans but he didn't recognise the white shirt or the thick navy jersey. She even seemed to be wearing a little makeup. Not that he was an expert on such matters. Whatever, he thought she looked very beautiful.

'It is chilly and grey, but I wonder if you'd like to take a walk before we do the shopping. I sometimes walk along Årstaviken. It's beautiful along the water and if the sun makes the briefest appearance, that's where you catch it.'

She nodded in acceptance and Otto held the front door open for her to pass.

OTTO WAS RIGHT. The sun did break through the clouds and as they walked along the shore it began to feel much warmer. The willows that leaned out over the water's edge had small pale-green leaves, and ducks swam peacefully in and out among the branches. A few boats were upended on the shore, but most of them were tied to the buoys on the water, awaiting summer adventures. A faint smell of tar and paint drifted on the air.

'I haven't seen Elias for a week or so. Usually he pops in a couple of times a week. I guess he's busy with his project.'

'I haven't seen him either. I haven't talked to him since . . . Well, since he invited me to come and take a closer look at his drawings.'

Otto threw her an interested glance.

'And what did you think?'

She didn't respond straight away.

'I am frightened by them.'

'Frightened?'

'Yes, they feel too close to me. Too personal. It's as if Elias has drawn my life. But it might just be me reading something into them that he never intended.' She squinted against the sun that played on the dark surface of the water.

'Does it matter? I mean, does it matter if it was his intention to draw what you think you see?'

'I think so. For him. And for me. I felt I had to tell him that I could read his story in the drawings, and that it is also my story.'

They walked in silence for a while, arm in arm.

'Elias asked me if I can write.'

'Yes?'

'And I had to say no. I can't write this story. It is absolutely impossible.'

'But if you can see it, hear it so clearly? Could you not at least try to write it?'

She shook her head.

'No, it's just not possible. I can't. I've tried to explain it to him. I hope he can understand.'

'I know hardly anything about you, Elisabeth, and as you know I don't speculate about other people and their lives. But when I read the books you have given me, and listen to you talking, I have the impression that you must be able to write. And do it beautifully.'

'It's one thing to be able to express yourself reasonably well. And to read other people's texts and take something from them. It's a totally different thing to write the words that Elias needs. Totally different.'

'Well, I wouldn't for the life of me be able to write creatively or poetically. Yet books have been my life. When I think about it, I realise I've written precious little in my life. Not since my school days. I've never even kept a diary.'

'I have,' said Elisabeth. 'All these years. Now I wonder why. But it felt like I understood things better if I wrote them down. As if my thoughts underwent some kind of process during the transfer from my brain to the paper. I imagined that it gave my thoughts a little order. But I wonder now if it wasn't all an illusion.'

'Why do you think that? I think it sounds very plausible. I

wish I had given it a try. Could it not also be a way of retaining the moments? Some thoughts are so transient. And others take up so much space that something has to be sacrificed in order to accommodate them. I've thought about this a lot lately. How much of my life has left no memories at all. Nothing. And I am talking about years, Elisabeth. Years that were presumably filled with experiences. And not a trace! I find it so sad.'

'Are you so certain they are irrevocably lost? This writing things down — I'm not so sure that it serves any purpose. It's a bit like taking a photo. You catch what you're focusing on, but that's all. But you might be focusing on the wrong things entirely. There's also the danger that what is written down somehow overshadows the memory. And later, when deciding which version to believe, we tend to choose the written one. Either way, you cannot hold on to everything.'

'Still, I envy you those diaries.'

Elisabeth smiled.

'I have given something to Elias. He might ask you to help him read it.'

Otto looked at her, a little surprised.

'Well, I decided I needed to try to explain to him why I can't write his text. Why I can't write at all. So I've given him the only thing I have ever written. When he gets to read it I think that he will understand. I hope so.'

'Of course I'll help him. But I'll wait and see if he asks. I don't want to intrude. Can I ask what it is that you have written?'

'It's a manuscript. A film script,' Elisabeth said, and there was a finality to the way she said it that made Otto know he shouldn't ask anything further.

They went up the slope along the Eriksdal swimming pools.

'Do you like swimming?' Otto asked and pointed to the building.

'I do, but I prefer to do it outdoors.'

'The outdoor pools are over there, on the other side. I usually go there in the morning during the summer and swim a few lengths. I make myself believe it's good for body and soul. I haven't got around to it yet this year.'

When they reached the top of the hill, Elisabeth stopped.

'I need to buy one of those USB memory sticks,' she said.

'There is a shop in there that sells things like that,' Otto said, pointing to the large shopping centre over the road. They waited for the traffic lights to change, then made their way across.

———————

ALL THE WAY BACK from the shop Otto thought about how to prolong their encounter without being too obvious. He offered to carry Elisabeth's shopping bags, but she insisted on doing it herself.

'It is good for me, Otto. A little exercise.'

It was lunchtime, but he didn't think lunch would be the right thing to suggest. They had been out for over two hours. She probably wanted a rest. Not that she looked tired; quite the opposite. He'd never seen her looking so alert. He slackened his pace and they walked slowly in the pale green shade under the chestnut trees in the churchyard. He couldn't make it last indefinitely; he realised that. They would soon be back home, and there was nothing he could do to change that.

'Thank you, Otto,' she said when they stood outside her door. 'It's been a nice morning.'

Otto gave a pleased smile.

'Yes, it has. And it looks like the sun is back. It's quite pleasant again.'

She lingered, as if there was something she wanted to add, but then seemed to change her mind.

'Well, thank you again. See you soon.'

They stood facing each other, shopping bags in their hands. Otto couldn't think of anything more to say.

'Yes, see you soon! Bye for now.'

27

THERE WAS NO LONGER any darkness. The nights were translucent, devoid of blackness. However hard she tried to recreate the dark, the treacherous light seeped through. She lay fully dressed on her bed. The bird on the wall appeared to be moving its little wings in small, desperate flaps. So hopelessly. So utterly hopelessly.

In her thoughts, she examined the events of the past few days. When she got to the hardest — the happiest moments — her stomach knotted and her heart beat as if in cramp. When she had watched Elias observe his own image in the mirror and slowly turn to her, smiling. Otto's arm around her shoulders. His lips on her hair. The laughter. Imagine that, laughter!

What had come over her? Not only had she responded to their initiatives, she had taken some herself.

'You leave me here, alone, in the shadows, Elisabeth.'

The Woman in Green was only just visible in the prevailing dusk. But her sadness filled the entire apartment.

'I am here too,' Elisabeth whispered.

'You come and you go. You have to make up your mind.'

'I have made up my mind. You know I have.'

The Woman in Green shook her head mournfully.

'You keep changing your mind, Elisabeth. You begin to hope. You turn away from me.'

'But you disappear,' Elisabeth said, choking on her tears. 'I can't see you any more.'

———

SHE AWOKE WITH THE afternoon sun on her face. When she stood up she felt dizzy and sat back down on the edge of the bed for a moment. Then everything poured forth again.

Her mad actions. Why had she interfered in Elias's life? Not just with his drawings, but his private life, too. She shook her head in disbelief.

I am absolutely mad. How could I ever imagine that I could help anybody, when I can't help myself?

Still, she couldn't shake the feeling that it had been the right thing to do. She saw Elias in her mind, and thought she could see all the possibilities that lay before him.

Then her manuscript. The most holy. The thing she had carried close to her chest in place of the child she never had, the life she had never lived. She now realised that all the other things she had brought with her to this place had just been padding — around the manuscript. Now she had given it to this young man who couldn't even read. What had she thought he would be able to do with it?

She went to the bathroom to have a shower.

Her wet hair wrapped in a towel, she sat down at the kitchen table with her laptop. The familiar desktop image appeared on the screen. Familiar and yet so strange. Like something belonging to another time, another life. She reached for the memory stick that Elias had given her, which had sat on top of the pile of mail since that evening. She watched the folder appear on the screen. Opened it and clicked on the images, one at a time, allowing them to cover the full screen. She examined them carefully, one by one. When she had finished she shut down the computer.

She stood up and went to dress. Then she took out a bottle of wine from the fridge, left the kitchen and walked out the front door.

———————

'I THOUGHT IT MIGHT be you. Even if I didn't quite allow myself to hope it would be,' Otto said as he opened the door.

Elisabeth held out the bottle. Ignoring it, Otto pulled her to him and held her close, inhaling the scent from her damp hair. Eventually he forced himself to let her go.

'I felt a little lonely, and it's another one of those beautiful evenings. And then I heard the blackbird. Can I come in for a bit?'

'My dear Elisabeth, you may stay as long as you like. You have no idea how happy I am to see you.'

He took the outstretched bottle and closed the door behind her.

'You've only really seen my kitchen. Shall we go and sit in the living room? But first, let's see if there is anything edible in the fridge. You haven't eaten, have you?' Elisabeth shook her head and Otto rubbed his hands together, pleased at the prospect of preparing food for her again.

'I wasn't going to bother cooking something just for me. But let's see . . .' He opened the fridge and started taking things out. In a few moments he had filled a tray with small bowls of olives, roasted almonds and hummus, toasted pita bread and sliced tomatoes and cucumber.

'Shall I boil a couple of eggs?' he asked.

Elisabeth shook her head.

'This is more than enough. I didn't really come to eat . . .'

Otto took the tray and led the way to the living room and Elisabeth followed, carrying the wine and two glasses.

It was more or less what Elisabeth had expected. Cosy and clearly lived in, a touch over-furnished and with overfull bookcases covering two of the walls. Near the window were hung several watercolours depicting dreamlike landscapes. Otto noticed that she had stopped to look at them.

'Those are Eva's paintings. I used to see them just as extensions of Eva herself. Now I realise that they are both beautiful and skilfully executed — works of art. I wish I had noticed that earlier. And I wish I had let her know.'

Elisabeth sat down on the green sofa and Otto took a seat in a very well-used armchair. There was no TV in the room, but Elisabeth spotted a sound system. It looked new and sophisticated. Again, she was reminded of how long it was since she had really listened to music.

'Music?'

She nodded. 'You choose.'

Without hesitation, Otto inserted a CD into the player.

He returned to his chair and poured the wine.

The music filled the room and Elisabeth rested her head on the back of the sofa and closed her eyes. When she opened them again she met Otto's eyes and realised he had been watching her.

'Do you like it?' he asked, as though her response genuinely mattered to him.

'It's very beautiful. But also very sad.'

'Yes, it is. It's a trio, of course.' He smiled a little embarrassed smile. 'Ever since we had that first dinner, the three of us, and I played Rachmaninov's Piano Trio No. 1, I have kept listening to trios. I had no idea there are so many. It's funny, really, because I have never listened to trios before. Quartets, yes. Sonatas, all kinds of chamber music. But not trios. Now I am discovering them, one after another. It's exciting, because in the small group each instrument is indispensable. Every note. And nothing can be disguised. The three musicians are so exposed, so completely dependent on each other. I appreciate it more and more. This is Tchaikovsky's Piano Trio in A minor, the first movement. It's like an echo of the Rachmaninov. Or perhaps it is rather the other way around, because apparently Rachmaninov was so impressed by Tchaikovsky's work that he wrote his first trio in celebration of it. I tell myself I can hear that. That the two pieces somehow respond to each other. But what do I know? I just listen and absorb.'

They listened to the music and picked at the food on the tray. Otto had lit a candle on the coffee table and the flame flickered in the cool evening air wafting from the open window.

Suddenly Otto placed his glass on the table. He leant forward, arms resting on his thighs and hands clasped between his knees, and looked up at Elisabeth.

'I have been thinking about that manuscript you have given to Elias. I haven't heard from him. Perhaps I'll never get to see it, if he decides to try to read it himself. For my sake, I hope not, because now I just can't stop thinking about you, Elisabeth. I have so many questions and I think they will be answered in that document.'

She looked at him, her head to one side.

'You don't need to worry. I'm sure he will ask you to read it. Even if he gives it a try himself first I think he'll want to share it with you. Because he'll need your help interpreting it. And when you have read it, if you still have questions you're welcome to ask me. If you're still wondering.'

'I don't wonder, really, Elisabeth. I worry.'

'Come here and sit by me,' said Elisabeth.

Otto slowly stood, walked around the coffee table and sat down on the sofa.

Elisabeth turned to him.

'You mustn't worry about me, Otto.' She placed her arms around his neck and kissed him on the cheek. Her face was very serious as she looked at him. 'I don't want you to worry at all. You have such a capacity for love and joy, and it would be such a waste of time if you spent it worrying about me.'

Otto tenderly placed a hand behind her neck. He pulled her towards him and kissed her on the mouth.

When she slowly released herself and stood up, he looked at her with a bewildered expression. During an endless moment he was afraid he had misinterpreted the signs. That she was leaving.

But she pulled him to his feet.

'Where is your bedroom?'

He gently lifted a wisp of her hair from her forehead and tucked it behind her ear. All the while his eyes were locked on hers.

'Are you sure?'

She held his gaze.

'I am absolutely sure, Otto. Absolutely sure.'

28

IT WAS MIDSUMMER AND a long week of brilliant summer weather was in prospect. But Elias had no interest in the weather. Not the Stockholm weather, anyway.

Midsummer had always been a holiday he had feared, back when it was just him and his mother. Long before he consciously understood it, he had registered his mother's bitterness over the fact that they had nowhere to go. When 'everybody else', those with whom she normally did not want to socialise or even acknowledge, had summer places to go to. She had nothing apart from her resentment to offer him, and the holiday used to drag itself along with no fixed points in the endlessness. No excursions, no visits, no festive lunches or dinners. Just a cold, clenched bitterness. Weekdays were better than holidays.

Later, when he started school, he soon learned that midsummers like his were not just lonely, but also shameful. A fact to be hidden at any cost. Although he had always realised that other people's midsummers were different, it was not until he met Maja that he understood how other people celebrated the holiday.

But by then his mother had met and married Gunnar, and the prevailing mood had gone from bitterness and resentment to fear. At first there was hope. With Gunnar they would start a new life in which everything they had missed out on would now come their way. Finally, the injustices would be corrected, the shame to be replaced by well-deserved pride.

But this period of hope had been very brief. The midsummers of endless loneliness became violent, drunken bouts, days to fear and to flee from.

When Elias left home, Maja's midsummers became his. And not just her midsummers, but her entire life. It became the life he used as a mirror. Yet he never became more than a reflection. Although he came to share so much with Maja, the life she had with her family could never be his, however kind and generous they were.

Then Otto appeared on the scene and the last few years they had shared the Midsummer's Eve dinner. It was not exactly a celebration. Elias had never asked, but he had the impression that Otto had a history of unhappy midsummers, too.

This midsummer would be different. Perhaps this was when the new life would begin. He couldn't help smiling as he stood in his living room, thinking about the week ahead.

He felt a stab of guilt when he thought of Otto. They had not specifically discussed Midsummer's Eve, but perhaps he was assuming they would spend it together as usual? He had to sort this out before he left.

He glanced at the pile of paper on the desk. He had made no attempt to read Elisabeth's manuscript, but merely paced in circles around it. Lifted a few sheets and put them back again. Examined the cover sheet as if he would be able to absorb the text just by boring his gaze into the pile.

He stepped around the suitcase that sat open on the floor and walked to the kitchen to fetch a plastic shopping bag. Back at his desk he pushed the manuscript into the bag and placed it on the doormat in the hallway.

It was hard to know what to pack. Paris. Provence. He'd been to Paris a few times to meet his publisher but he'd never stayed long enough to explore the city and get to know it. Now he would meet

Paul in Paris and stay with him for a few days. Then the two of them would travel on to the country house Paul's parents owned near Marseille.

'Don't worry — they'll love you. Mum speaks better English than I do, and Dad's is pretty good. Mum is a translator and Dad is a marine biologist. They are well travelled — quite decent people, actually. They love me, their only child. And they love those that I love.' Elias caught the nuance that there had been many before him. But then Paul had laughed and hugged him. And Elias had laughed, too.

He threw in a few more t-shirts. Then he went to the door and picked up the plastic bag.

———

OTTO OPENED THE DOOR and threw a quick glance at the bag in Elias's hand.

'Come in, come in,' he said, stepping aside to let Elias enter.

They went and sat at the kitchen table. Otto had not started cooking, but a faint smell drifted in from the courtyard below where someone was using the barbecue.

Elias placed the bag on the table.

'You already know what it is, don't you?' he said.

Otto nodded.

'I haven't even read the letter. It's like I've been walking around it in ever-decreasing circles for several days. Staring at it as if it would explain itself to me without my having to struggle through it. It didn't work.' He smiled a crooked smile and handed Otto the folded letter. Otto took his time unfolding it and reached for his glasses.

He read in silence. In the stillness they could hear the voices of the people down in the courtyard.

'Would you like me to read it to you?' Otto asked when he had finished.

'Yes. Would you?'

'It's addressed to you, of course.' He began to read.

Dear Elias,

I know how difficult it is for you to read, so you might rightly wonder why I am giving you this. There is no need to read any further, but I think Otto would be happy to help you if that is what you want. I'm leaving this in your hands now. I don't want it back. You are free to do with it what you want.

I feel I owe you a kind of explanation. You know how I dislike owing anybody anything. So, here it is.

You asked me if I can write. I said no, and I meant it. I was able to write once, I think. As far back as I can remember I have kept a diary but that's not exactly literary writing. Occasionally, I suppose, diary writing turns into beautiful or moving literature. But that is not the case with my diary.

My diary was a way of trying to understand my existence. When I wrote down my experiences and my thoughts they became more comprehensible. So, my diaries were just for me. Then I came to work with the words of others. I became an actress. When I was at drama school I found there were many people like me there. People who needed the words of others in order to feel alive. But more than anything, what I learnt there was the treacherous feeling of comfort that comes from acting other people's lives rather than living your own. It took me a very long time to realise that when I left the school I kept this up. I continued to live other people's lives. I don't think I even knew who the real me was.

This manuscript, Elias, is the only thing I have written for anyone other than myself. It is a film script, but it was hardly read, and was never made into a film. Not in the way that I might have hoped, anyway. I wrote it in a kind of desperation, I can see that now. You must understand, Elias, that I had reached a point in my life when everything that had filled my life had been lost. Had simply vanished into nothing. I was totally naked and exposed.

Perhaps I thought this script would lead me to something new. Open a new door, or at least make me see that I could hope for something more. As I wrote it, I came to hope that it would develop into something usable.

I chose Strindberg's The Inferno *from Otto's bookshelf. I read it a long time ago but I don't think I understood it. Now I like to think I do. But it doesn't really matter whether I understand it in the way that Strindberg imagined it. The text has a meaning for me — it speaks to me. This is what Strindberg writes:*

'There occur in life incidents so horrible that the soul refuses to keep the impression of them at that moment, but the impression remains and soon re-emerges with irresistible power.'

That is exactly how it is, Elias. At first you believe that there is a new door, and that you can open it. That there is a future, something worth exploring. But my text didn't open a new door. Nor was it able to close the old one. Quite the opposite, one might say. It left me hanging in the void between the two. And there, Elias, there is absolutely nothing.

I don't know why I have carried this pile of paper for so long. It has no value at all to anybody. And now I simply cannot carry it any more. So, here it is. I give it to you, Elias. Feel free to set fire to it. Throw it in the rubbish. But I thought that if you read my manuscript you might understand that it is not that I can't write per se. But that I can't write any more.

Elisabeth

When he finished Otto refolded the letter, thinking about its contents.

'Of course I'd be happy to read it,' he said. 'Delighted. I've been looking forward to it, I might as well admit. You see, I have become . . . well, very fond of Elisabeth. And I think this will be important to my understanding of her.' He placed his palm on the manuscript. 'Reading it feels like a privilege as well as a responsibility. Not just for me, for both of us.'

'Yes. It's connected to my images in some way. How, I don't understand. But somehow it is.'

'A beer? Or a glass of wine?' Otto stood up.

'A beer, please. Thank you.'

Otto opened the fridge and handed Elias a beer. He poured himself a glass of wine and sat down again.

'I actually came up to tell you I'm flying to Paris tomorrow,' Elias said.

'Really? Is it work?'

Elias shook his head and couldn't hold back a self-conscious smile.

'No. I've met someone. His name is Paul and he lives in Paris. He's a photographer — a very good one, I think. And . . . well, he's invited me to stay with him over midsummer. A few days at his place in Paris, then a week with his parents in Provence. I'll be gone almost two weeks.'

Otto smiled and took both of Elias's hands in his.

'I am so very happy for you, Elias. Take care. But dare to embrace this, too. This thing called love is complicated. Because that's what it is about, isn't it?'

Elias nodded.

'Without love, life is not worth very much. Words of wisdom from an old man who has gained some insight very late in life.' He laughed.

Elias looked at Otto. He wondered if he had ever heard him laugh in that way before. He had always seemed content, but this heartfelt laughter — it felt new.

'Cheers, and happy midsummer, Otto.'

'Cheers, Elias. To love!'

29

OTTO SAT AT THE kitchen table with the manuscript in front of him. He'd not started on the text but he'd read the letter several times. He stood up and paced the hallway. He was gripped by an inexplicable feeling of anxiety. He was afraid to open the manuscript. Afraid in the same way that he had been to run his hands over Elisabeth's skin. Kiss the small dent at the base of her throat and inhale her perfume. She felt so delicate, so utterly fragile. He felt clumsy and insecure, but she led him on. And in a way this letter did the same. It encouraged him to read on, to learn her most intimate secrets. But he was afraid of what he would find out. And he was afraid of the finality of the letter. It sounded like a farewell.

He cautiously lifted the cover page and read the title:

Broken Wings

And so he turned the page and began to read. He'd never read a film script before, and to begin with he found it hard to ignore the stage directions and get inside the story itself. But after a few scenes he was completely absorbed.

OTTO LOWERED THE PAGE he had just read. He removed his glasses and pinched the top of his nose hard. He took a sip of wine and stared unseeing out the window. He wasn't sure he wanted to read on.

He went into his bedroom and turned on the computer. Opened Google and typed the search words *broken* and *wings* and *film*.

There were many hits — too many for him to check them all. He clicked on what looked like a review. Then another, and another. The reviewers were not kind. Otto knew little about film, and even less about French film. This one seemed to have been a total fiasco, but he couldn't be sure it was the same film.

Broken Wings appeared to have been an EU production, with a French director called David Abelin and starring a young British actress, apparently married to the director.

Otto kept clicking away and it became clear that David Abelin had a fine track record: seven films that had achieved both artistic recognition and public success.

Then he found Elisabeth.

Elisabeth Abelin, actress. Young. Heartbreakingly beautiful. And a marriage held up as a perfect example of a union between two artists: a director and his muse. The celebrated French film director and his beautiful, talented, Swedish actress wife. A golden couple.

Otto stared into the screen.

And there it was:

With Broken Wings *David Abelin has broken his distinguished track record. In the past he has chosen his scripts with such care, but something seems to have gone very wrong this time. The script, written for the first time by the director himself, is strangely lopsided, and in parts incomprehensible.*

Perhaps the biggest problem is the disastrous miscasting of the female lead, the young British actress Jennifer Caulston. The female roles that Abelin has previously created, portrayed so memorably by his then wife Elisabeth Abelin, have all impressed with their realism and multi-faceted depth — both completely lacking in this film.

There is clearly an interesting story somewhere in there. A story that could have made a fascinating study of the marriage between two creative people, its gradual erosion and final collapse. Since Abelin separated from his previous wife immediately before the production of Broken Wings, *it is difficult to escape the conclusion that the film was intended as a commentary on the director's own situation. But with the young and inexperienced Caulston in the lead role, and a script that gives the part little dramatic space, this intention was far from realised. It is hard not to grieve for the film that could have been.*

———————

IT WAS EARLY MORNING when Otto turned the last page of the script. Already daylight when he turned off the lamp. He removed his glasses and rubbed his eyes. He had wept several times, but he had kept reading to the end.

He rose and stood by the window. Took a few deep breaths and regarded the sky above the rooftops. It would be another fine day.

He turned and looked back at the manuscript on the table. This was the first dramatic script he had ever read so he was not able to judge whether it was good or bad, but he knew it contained material that should have been able to make an exceptional film. He couldn't understand how it could have gone so disastrously wrong.

Notwithstanding his relationship with Elisabeth — if he dared to call it a relationship, and if he could honestly say that he was able to put aside something that occupied him so completely — this material was extraordinary. He couldn't understand how someone could write about something so intimate and so obviously painful, and yet maintain a sort of objectivity, a distance from the story. Regard herself with such terrible honesty.

The mere thought moved him to tears again.

He was absolutely convinced it was her own story. Could it perhaps have started as a diary? An attempt at making her existence understandable? Something to hold on to when everything else slipped from her hands?

This was how it felt to him. Elisabeth was telling her story with a clear-eyed impartiality and brutal honesty that was so infinitely moving. But it also felt as if the story had an underlying personal purpose. As if she laid open their entire relationship and its tragic collapse for her own sake. In order to force herself to see all its sordid detail. She was not apportioning blame; she wanted to try to understand. So she could give her life a different direction and create a foundation for something new. So by understanding the past she would be able to see the future.

It also seemed she was trying to make a personal tragedy universally relevant.

He simply could not accept that a film based on this script — Elisabeth's script — could have been so very bad. But hadn't the review said that Elisabeth's former husband, the director himself, wrote the script? Otto was confused.

His gaze fell on the small glass container where he kept odd little bits and pieces like batteries, matches, rubber bands and paper clips. And Elisabeth's key.

He had not given it much thought when she gave it to him. He had just assumed that she felt he could be trusted to keep a spare key for emergencies. He had one also for Elias's apartment, and Elias had his. A practical arrangement.

Now, he wondered if she had meant something more in giving it to him. He tried to remember exactly what she had said. This was when she had kissed him the first time. But what had she said?

'Just in case.'

At the time he had not read anything particular into those words, but now he wondered. There were several possible inter-pretations. Otto was suddenly filled with a gnawing anxiety.

If Elisabeth's script was autobiographical — and he had no reason to believe otherwise — then she had ended up here as a last resort. He saw her in his mind as a damaged bird, washed ashore from a stormy sea. A bird with a broken wing, barely alive.

He had no experience himself of being betrayed and abandoned. He had never felt he belonged with anybody else, or that anybody else belonged with him. And in order to be abandoned, he now realised, you had to feel that belonging. He understood that there were those who felt so intimately tied to their loved one that life lost all meaning when they were abandoned, whether through death or infidelity or some other betrayal. He knew this, but he had never experienced it. All he had experienced was a vague sadness and loneliness. And a physical emptiness, as when his hand searched for Eva's body in his sleep. But he had felt no overwhelming grief nor anger. A vague sadness and loneliness, that was all.

What Elisabeth was describing was something entirely different. A kind of love he had never known, and a betrayal so terrible that he had found it difficult to read about. It was not death that robbed Elisabeth of her love. In a sense, you could say it was life.

He wondered if it was not in a sense less difficult to lose your loved one to death. Absolute and non-negotiable, death is something you are forced to accept as best you can. Death can arrive at any time and it shows no mercy. It can be a drawn-out process preceded by dreadful suffering, or it can come like a bolt out of the blue. But death is a third party. Objective in its complete ruthlessness. It tears the lovers apart, but they themselves are not parties to the act. Whatever death might be, it is never deceitful. Never scheming. You can't negotiate with death; you can't plea or beg. And death never changes its mind.

While he was with Eva it had never even entered his mind to have an affair with anyone else. Nor had he thought that Eva might do so. He suddenly realised that she could very well have entertained the idea — even acted on it. He would never know.

He knew that it was common, of course. He had recently read that almost half of all Swedish marriages ended in divorce. And infidelity occurred in many marriages that were not dissolved. Infidelity was not necessarily the ultimate betrayal.

No, the ultimate betrayal was the deliberate destruction of the dependent party. The one who loved more.

You cannot force someone to love, or to remain in a relationship. Elisabeth's main story might seem more interesting than some of its kind — at least to his eyes — but its essence was just a version of the oldest story of all. It was about falling in love. Being in love. And falling out of love. Otto felt that there was a strange kind of beauty in all three parts. The story was carried by such a strong sense of, well, of love, actually. Even in the last part, there was so much love. And a measure of hope. Not hope for the relationship, but a fragile hope of a future.

He stood in the centre of the kitchen, unable to decide what to do. He sat down again and turned over some leaves at random.

E.   I had thought that love would be light as a feather, yet stronger than anything else. I had thought I would be able to place my entire self in his hands and feel safe. Just as he would be able to place himself in my hands and know that I would protect him with my life.

Yes, I was naïve, but not so naïve that I didn't understand that there would be challenges. But I did believe that inside, in our innermost selves, we would keep each other safe. However much it might storm around us. It is strange how easy it is to project your own hopes onto others, and make yourself believe that they are theirs, too.

It is equally strange how long it takes before you begin to realise that you have been mistaken. That nobody at all has carried you inside.

And yet it can be so very difficult to tear out what you have carried. In spite of the insight. It is as if it has fused with your body. Your heart and your lungs. Your brain has nothing to do with it, of course. The fact that the person you have carried inside you has become a part of you and can no longer be separated from you: it has nothing to do with logic. It just happens.

However heavy the burden has become, and however clearly you realise you ought to let it go, and however essential it is to try to protect yourself, you just cannot rid yourself of it. It is impossible.

And yet there is nobody carrying you any more.

You cease to exist, quite simply.

30

ELISABETH FOUND THE NOTE on her doormat in the early morning the day before Midsummer's Eve.

> *Dear Elisabeth*
> *It seems we will be blessed with one of the rarest occasions this year:*
> *A Midsummer's Eve with perfect summer weather. The predictions are*
> *for clear skies tomorrow, no wind and temperatures well over 20°C.*
> *It would make me very happy if you would spend it with me. I will*
> *prepare something to eat, but I thought we could go for a long walk*
> *before we eat. If it suits you, I will pick you up after lunch. Say, about*
> *2pm? Let me know if another time would be better.*
> *Your*
> *Otto*

She smiled and read the note again. He had surprisingly young and driven handwriting. He wrote with ink, and the paper was of high quality. The result was beautiful, quite irrespective of the message.

She folded the note carefully and placed it on the table. But not on the pile of unopened mail.

In fact the pile was no longer there. She had stuffed it all into a plastic bag and put it by the front door. She knew it contained no bills because everything was paid by the trust fund. The fund that had existed in the background all her life, but that she had never used. She had already met David when she turned twenty-one and gained control over the money her parents had left behind. She didn't need it, so the money was kept invested. But now she was grateful — not for the money as such, but for being able to leave the practical responsibilities to others.

She had created a simple workplace on the table. The laptop was open and waiting. She sat down and placed her hand on the mouse, and watched the screen light up. There was the first image: the one that was on her bedroom wall.

A blackbird. Or just a small black bird. It lay on its side on what looked like dirty, wet snow. On the wall, she had thought she saw its small wings flap in despair. Looking at it closely here on the screen, every detail was even clearer and she thought she could see its tiny breast heave, its beak open as if struggling for air. A small feather had come loose and lay to the side. She wondered why she hadn't noticed that before. The eye stared upwards, towards an invisible sky. It was clear the bird was only just alive.

Elisabeth opened a new document. She hesitated for a moment with her fingers on the keys. Then she slowly typed the letters of the title:

The Blackbird

She sat staring at the empty white screen for a moment, fingers resting on the keyboard.

'I have no idea what I am doing,' she said to herself. 'I am not a writer, am I? Certainly not a poet. I already made that clear to you, Elias. Yet here I am. I will give it a try. I don't understand why. But I will try to write you a manuscript. A film script. I'm not sure what use you might find for it. If I do manage to write something.'

Before she began to type, she inserted a CD into the computer and placed the earphones in her ears.

WHEN SHE HAD FIRST arrived there had seemed to be no daylight at all. She had been able to lie in her bedroom enveloped in the soothing and forgiving uninterrupted darkness. And she had been able to follow the Woman in Green towards emptiness, gradually learning how to disable her senses. Rid herself of thoughts and feelings. Riding deeper and deeper into the darkness.

Now, there was no darkness at all, it seemed. When she looked up from the computer screen she was surprised to find that it was still bright daylight outside, although she knew it was late. She had spent all day at the computer, with only short breaks. It was surprising how easily the words had flowed. In a sense, she had written it all before, and now she was just adapting it, choosing the words more carefully, making the sentences more poignant. And perhaps also more generic, if such a thing was possible.

> B. A star. My eyes can see a star. That is all.
> One lonely little light in a vast darkness.
> If I close my eyes, will I smother it? The
> only light? The last light?
>
> E. No, my little one. When you open your
> eyes again you will see that the light seems
> brighter. And that it is not the only one.
>
> B. What if I cannot? If my eyes remain
> closed? What will happen to the star?
>
> E. This is difficult to know. Best to open
> your eyes.

She stood up and walked to the open window. All was still. She couldn't even discern any distant sounds. It was just her and the pale summer night.

She would find no peace. She was filled with a strange sense of urgency and she sat down again.

THE CHURCH BELLS STRUCK 4am when she finally turned off the computer. She was not tired; she just needed to leave the computer and the text. The process inside her head could not be switched off as easily, though.

She rinsed her face and brushed her teeth and went to the bedroom. She walked over to the drawing on the wall and leant forward for a closer look. Now she could see that there were subtle differences. She had been right. This bird had not lost a feather, and its eyes were closed. But everything else was exactly the same. Had he altered the original after giving her this copy? Or made an altered version? Or was it only in her imagination that the bird had come alive?

She undressed and lay down on the bed. For months she had avoided looking at herself in the mirror. Now, she ran her palms over her breasts. Cupped her hands around them. Ran one hand over the flat of her stomach. It was odd how unfamiliar it felt. As though it no longer belonged to her.

Otto had placed his hands on her skin with infinite gentleness, and she had felt a strange surge of vague recognition, a delicate stirring of something that had been asleep for a very long time. But it was when she ran her own hands over his chest, let her lips rest on his throat, and, ever so lightly, travel down his body, that the miracle happened. When she looked up and caught his eyes, those pools of amber light, and found them filled with absolute and astonished delight. Gratitude. And sheer joy. She had been overcome by a sudden rush of absolute happiness.

But now she was here, alone in her bedroom, while the morning spread over the city outside. It was the early hours of Midsummer's Eve. And that elusive moment of happiness seemed very distant.

The first rays of sun had reached the treetops across the street when she finally fell asleep. She did not hear the church strike five. Nor did she hear the blackbird begin to sing in the backyard.

31

OTTO INSPECTED HIS FACE in the mirror above the hand-basin. He often referred to himself as 'old' . . . 'an old man', but he had never really changed the way he viewed himself. He had just tried to adjust to the impression that he assumed he made on other people. He *was* old, but he did not *feel* old. Not young, either, for that matter. Just himself.

But now when he tried to view himself objectively he could definitely see signs of old age. The skin underneath his chin seemed to have lost its hold on the bones and hung in loose folds; the eyelids were wrinkled and he had to open his eyes wide in order to lift the lids completely. He had always had good teeth but they were no longer white.

He held up his hands and noted how thin and mottled the skin was. But when he placed the palm on his cheek and skin met skin, he was reminded of the sensation of placing his hand on Elisabeth's breast. Running it over her skin. Inhaling her perfume. The overwhelming sensation of her hands on his skin. Her lips. And the blood rush to his genitals.

'Here I am. Otto Vogel. I am sixty-eight years old. And I am in love.'

He stared at himself.

'It's a complete miracle. And even if this is all, even if I were to die this instant, I would do so knowing that life's greatest gift has been bestowed on me. A miracle.'

He turned off the light and left the bathroom. Today, he dressed with purpose. Everything was laid out ready. The new brown polo shirt and the beige chinos. He slipped his feet into the leather sandals and returned to the bathroom. He splashed some eau de cologne into his cupped hands and rubbed his palms over his cheeks and throat. He had acquired a new level of awareness. He was aware of every part of his body. His hands on his cheeks, the feeling of the new clothes on his body, his feet inside the sandals. Every tiny movement was filled with a new and deeper purpose, and all his senses were sharpened.

Closing the front door behind him, he stood in the stairwell and took a few deep breaths.

'Thank you,' he whispered. Asked to whom this was directed he would probably not have been able to answer. He had never been religious, never considered himself having a belief or the vision of a higher power, a god. He was just so filled with a sense of gratitude that he had to give thanks.

'Thank you.'

He set off down the stairs.

———

ELISABETH OPENED THE DOOR and Otto was speechless. She had clearly unpacked some more clothes he had not seen before. A low-cut coral-red blouse that left her neck and a bit of her shoulders bare, and white trousers. She looked at him with an expression that was difficult to interpret. A smile, perhaps, or a question? Or a bit of both?

'You look so beautiful, Elisabeth,' he said quietly.

Now she was definitely smiling.

'Thank you,' she said, and stepped outside, closing the door behind her. He placed his arm around her waist and inhaled the smell of her hair. He had an impulse to embrace her, lift her off her feet, shout with joy, but was uncertain of how she would react. While he was hesitating, she turned to face him, threw her arms around his neck and kissed him.

'Happy Midsummer, Otto!' she said. She took his hand in hers and they walked down the steps and out into the street.

THEY WALKED ARM IN arm and when they reached the crest of the railway bridge they stopped and looked out over the water. Lots of small boats dotted the surface below, on their way either up into Lake Mälaren, or down towards the lock that would take them out into the Baltic and the archipelago.

'Would you believe me if I told you I've never set foot on a yacht?'

'Why wouldn't I? Surely many haven't.' Elisabeth laughed.

'What about you?'

'Yes, I have sailed. Not as a child, but later, after I . . . My husband sailed. He had a beautiful yacht. And like most people who sail, he was passionate about it. About the boat, and about sailing. So I had to learn, and I came to love it as passionately as he did. I tried hard to learn to love all the things he loved, but with sailing it was never an effort. We never sailed here, in the cold and dark water of the north. We sailed in the Mediterranean, which is a very different matter. So we share this, you and I: neither of us has sailed here.'

'Yes, we do.' He was suddenly sombre. 'There is so much I have never tried. Never really understood, or even known about. My world seems so small now in retrospect. Maybe because my mother never really understood her new home country. Not in the way you do when your family has lived there for generations. She really tried. She wanted to embrace all things Swedish. But there's a difference between conscious effort and natural absorption. My mother and I learnt the superficial attributes but the real essence — of the holidays, for example — escaped us. Perhaps particularly so Midsummer. We ate herring and new potatoes and strawberries. And I remember my mother taking me to the local playground on Midsummer's Eve. With the others who were left in the city we congregated around a maypole. Someone played the accordion and we danced. But it was like being a tourist and participating in some exotic ritual.

'We never really owned the Midsummer, Mother and I, so it has never really bothered me that I have often spent it by myself, treating it like any other weekend. If Eva and I had had children, then perhaps things would have been different. Our children might have grasped the essence of Midsummer. And many other things, too. I sometimes think about that, and wonder if I would have grown deeper roots here if I had had children.'

He squinted against the sun and gazed down on the sea below.

'Where did your family come from?' asked Elisabeth.

'Vienna. You'd think that Austria would not be so very different from Sweden, but an abyss separates the two cultures. At the same time we're so very much alike. It's strange. Perhaps it has to do with expectations. If you move to a country that is obviously very different then you are prepared. You relate to it differently. Yet the differences that are the most difficult are the subtle ones. The things you cannot really put your finger on. As though there's an invisible fabric that unites the "real" citizens but is not accessible for the recent arrivals. As an immigrant you may learn the language perfectly, adopt all the habits and traditions, but it's never enough. You remain an immigrant — for generations, I think. Look at me, Elisabeth. Would you have thought I was a proper Swede?'

Elisabeth regarded him as if evaluating him.

'Hm, not sure. I know you now, so I can no longer see you objectively. You are an unusual man, that's for sure. Born and bred Swede or not.'

She laughed.

'But I know what you mean. I lived in France for over thirty years. So long that I forgot I wasn't really French. Then invariably, something would happen to remind me. It would be something I said or did. Or sometimes nothing at all. I would be addressed in English when I thought I blended in perfectly. But at some level it never really bothered me. I was always quite happy to be Swedish, however much I loved France. I had never actually emigrated, the way people do who are fleeing from war and terror. I just moved there to be with my French husband, for however long. I suppose I never regarded it as permanent. Strange, now that I think about it. Because I certainly regarded our relationship as being forever.'

She paused, as if considering what she had just said.

'He seemed to like it too, my Swedishness. At least during the early years. He'd introduce me as his Swedish wife — make a point of it. But my lack of understanding of French subtleties often annoyed him, and he used to laugh at my linguistic mistakes. I never, ever became French.'

Otto put his hand over hers on the railing in front of them.

'I lived in Vienna until I was almost six. I'm not sure if my memories of that time are really memories or just projections based on my mother's stories. I had a little sister, Elsa — I do remember her. And I like to think I have memories of my father. Not many, but enough to be convinced that he loved me.'

Otto offered his arm to Elisabeth and they carried on across the bridge.

'My father was in charge of the machinery at a large printing company. The staff who had specialist roles escaped the draft so I think both my parents felt very lucky. Our family was able to lead a relatively normal life, in spite of the war. But Elsa became very ill. My little sister didn't starve to death, and she wasn't killed by a bomb or a grenade or a gun. She just got ill. And she died. And after that my father began working longer and longer hours. Sometimes he didn't come home at all, but slept for a few hours at work. It became absolutely silent at home. I do remember that. In some way, I think I knew then that it was just Mother and me left.

'I don't know exactly what had happened, but one day the police came and told us that Father had been killed in an accident at work.

My mother never spoke about it. When she talked about my father it was memories of the earlier days. When we were a happy family. But this is probably not uncommon — wanting to give your child the happy memories only. And like I said, now I'm not sure if my memories of my father really are memories, or constructions after the fact. But I know my mother did her best to give me a loving father. And I think she succeeded.'

They walked in silence.

'It's so hard, this matter of our memories,' said Elisabeth. 'My parents died in a traffic accident when I was eight. My memories of them, of us together, are crystal clear. When it first happened, I used to think of us inside one of those snow globes, except that there was no snow, there was sunshine. Flakes of gold, and dazzlingly bright colours. And that's where we lived, the three of us. Outside, the world had no colours at all. And outside there was also my burning anger towards Mum and Dad who had left me behind. I ended up projecting this anger onto the only person who loved me: my aunt Anita, my father's older sister. Anita and her husband Krister took me in. They had no children of their own and I think Anita hoped I would become hers. That my first eight years would fade and eventually dissolve.

'But the harder she tried, the more I withdrew. The more I hated her. I didn't want to be the child she never had, I wanted to be the child of my parents. And most of all my mother's child. When I became a teenager it was awful. I didn't want their love. I didn't want to eat their food. I wanted nothing to do with their Christmases, Easters and Midsummers. I knew they really cared about me, and that Anita loved me. But the person they wanted to give their care and their love to wasn't me at all. Anita loved someone who didn't exist. And I . . . well, I had nobody to love.'

At the end of the bridge they used the overpass to cross the railway line and carry on along the water on the southern side.

'I remember the day I told them I wanted to be an actor. Like my mother. I remember that I felt a kind of hot satisfaction when I saw Anita's expression. It was as if I had given her a slap on the face. An actor! Their resistance was really genuine concern, I know that now. They wanted what was best for me, in their way. But they were never able to reach me. Now of course I know that the life my mum and dad led was not the life I had fantasised about. That the accident may not have been an accident. And that Anita and Krister wanted to protect me from that knowledge. But that's not how it felt then. My disgust just grew and grew. I felt like I couldn't breathe in their clean and tidy home where nothing ever changed. The monotony of their seasonal routines made me stiff with resentment. Winter skiing, summer at their country house, their holiday celebrations. Absolutely predictable and unchangeable from year to year. The same decorations, the same food, the same traditions. It seemed to be the fabric that held them together. I felt as if I would explode if I had to suffer another day of their life. So I fled. Found a sublease on a small flat in Jungfrugatan. I took odd jobs to manage, and somehow it worked out. There was no going back.'

They stopped to watch two small girls feeding bread to the ducks. The father held the bag and the little girls ran back and forth, giggling and shouting to each other.

'Then I was accepted into drama school — on my first try. And that's where I met my first real boyfriend, Mattias. He was everything I was not. He came from a family where they all seemed to be involved with the arts in one way or another. They were all completely supportive. Mattias was absolutely sure of what he wanted to achieve.

'As for me, the only thing I was absolutely sure of was what I did *not* want to do. I did not want to become like Anita and Krister. And I found that drama school gave me exactly that which I had missed: an identity. Well, not just *one* identity, but many. I didn't have to be anybody at all, which was wonderful. I realised that my ability to live a part was better than most. I could effortlessly pick up an accent, adopt gestures, facial expressions and body language. It was as if I only lived through the parts that I played.

'In my free time I was acting Mattias's muse — an infinitely accommodating, almost transparent figure. I had no firm ideas, no tastes of my own. But I felt safe in Mattias's company. He was . . . well, absent-mindedly accepting. I think he saw me as some kind of personal item — a garment, a jacket, perhaps. One he liked and which kept him warm, and at the same time demanded nothing of him. Something that was at hand as required. But — and this I think I knew all along — something that was replaceable. I'm not sure if I was ever in love with him. I was in love with his life. Fascinated by his visions and his dreams. I wanted him to dream for me, too, and let me tag along. So that I wouldn't have to think about what I wanted for myself.

'But then I met David. And in his world, someone like me was not safe at all. I was a possession for him, too, but the demands on me were severe and often difficult to understand. I tried really hard. I thought I'd learn to play the part perfectly if I only kept trying. But the demands kept changing and I could never keep up. It took me a very long time to understand that he never really wanted me to adapt. Go along with his ever harsher demands. He wanted me to stand up for myself. But by the time I realised that it was too late. For both of us.'

The walkway had meandered up the hill past the small allotment gardens. There were a few others out and about: walking their dogs, jogging. For long stretches they were alone. Otto held Elisabeth's hand in his.

'Do you know this is the first time I have held a woman's hand like this?'

He lifted their hands.

'Another first for me: walking side by side with a woman and holding her hand in mine.'

Elisabeth looked at him, her eyebrows raised.

'Yes, I'm sure you find that odd,' Otto continued, 'but it's true. Eva was not like that. Sometimes we walked arm in arm, but usually we just walked side by side. It never felt natural to take her hand. I have no idea why, when it is the most natural thing in the world. And so very . . . well, so very satisfying.'

He smiled.

————

BACK IN OTTO'S APARTMENT everything was laid out for their dinner. Glasses, plates and cutlery sat in a basket on the kitchen table.

'I took a punt on the weather holding up, and since we're probably the only people left in the building we'll have the courtyard to ourselves. So I suggest we eat down there.'

Elisabeth nodded in agreement.

'Glass of wine?'

Elisabeth took the glass he offered and Otto poured the chilled white wine.

'The usual toast?'

'The usual toast.'

They raised their glasses and looked into each other's eyes. Otto placed his hand at the back of Elisabeth's neck and pulled her gently to him. He put his cheek against hers and held her.

'This morning I took a long, hard look at myself in the mirror. To try to see what I might look like to others. And most important, how I might look to you. But you know, Elisabeth, I couldn't make any sense of it. I could *see* what I looked like, but it was like my eyesight was no longer connected to my brain. Why is that?'

Elisabeth took a step back to get a proper look at him. She smiled and shook her head.

'I don't know, Otto. You tell me.'

'Well, you see, I am just so completely busy being happy. You shouldn't really swear in the company of a lady, but you know, Elisabeth, I really don't give a damn about how I look — I am just so very happy!'

Elisabeth laughed.

'You're crazy, Otto. But I do think you are beautiful. Inside and out.'

'To you, possibly,' he said, blushing a little.

He placed his glass on the table, pulled her close again and kissed her.

———

IT TOOK THEM TWO trips to carry everything down to the courtyard. Otto spread a white tablecloth over the garden table and set it with fine china and crystal glasses. He had prepared poached salmon in aspic and a salad with new potatoes, asparagus and snow peas. Elisabeth suspected that the bread rolls were homemade, too, like the mayonnaise. They sat opposite each other and they were just about to eat when Otto jumped up again. He walked over to the large old lilac tree, which was covered in heavy clusters of open flowers. He picked a few stems and placed them at the centre of the table.

'I think we should have some decorations,' he said and sat down again.

Elisabeth was overcome by a sense of being alone in an abandoned city. She pictured the way they might look from high above. Their small courtyard framed by lilacs and the old linden tree by the wall. The small table set with food and wine. And Otto there, beside her. The city had closed its eyes, turned its back to them, and they were free to do whatever they fancied. She smiled to herself. Suddenly she had a vision of the snow globe of her childhood. But this one had the two of them, her and Otto, contained inside the globe and surrounded by slowly falling flecks of gold.

'What are you thinking about?'

Elisabeth turned the wine glass in her hand.

'Oh, nothing really. That's what is so extraordinary.'

Otto held out his glass and looked at her. She lifted her glass and met his gaze.

'This is our moment, Elisabeth. Our time, finally.'

———

MUCH LATER, WHEN THE sunny day had become warm evening and finally cool night, they had returned upstairs. Otto sat on the sofa, his legs stretched out and his feet on a footstool. Elisabeth lay along the sofa beside him, her head on his lap. His fingers played absent-mindedly with wisps of her hair.

'This is what I was waiting for all those years. The perfect Midsummer's Eve. Now I know it was worth waiting for.'

Elisabeth smiled without opening her eyes.

———

OTTO WOKE UP. He couldn't tell what had woken him. He carefully turned onto his side and regarded her. She lay curled up, one hand stuck underneath the pillow. He let his eyes run over her face, her neck and the half-visible breast. And he realised that it was happiness that had woken him, and he could not allow himself to sleep away any more of it.

He lay perfectly still, breathing slowly and soundlessly. He could hear no sounds from outside either, even though the window was wide open. The fine curtain barely moved in the soft breaths of air that found their way inside. He held his hands clasped so that he would not give in to the temptation to stretch out an arm and place his hand somewhere on her skin. He could see her eyes flickering underneath her eyelids and assumed she must be dreaming. She didn't look sad or worried. In fact her face wore a serene expression.

Pure and innocent, he thought. This is mine. This moment will always belong to me.

The faint first notes of the blackbird wafted in through the window.

Otto smiled. Just when he had thought nothing could be added to this moment.

He kept his eyes steadily on her face as the birdsong lifted between the walls of the buildings.

And she opened her eyes.

32

ELIAS STOOD IN THE centre of the room, looking towards the open window. He had just showered. It had become full summer in his absence, even though he'd been away less than two weeks. It seemed appropriate that so much had happened here, since so much had happened to him in that short time span.

He shifted his gaze to the suitcase that lay open at his feet, filled with new clothes. It felt like he had shed a skin. It hadn't been painful but it had been overwhelming. Huge. And somehow a little frightening. It was scary to be this happy.

Stepping inside the apartment had felt like stepping back into a bygone time.

He started sorting his clothes, throwing things into the laundry bag. Then he closed the suitcase and put it at the back of the wardrobe. He pulled on a pair of jeans and a t-shirt from the pile of clean clothes and put the rest away.

It was with a strange feeling of trepidation that he sat down at his desk and opened the laptop.

The first image.

His instant reaction was relief. He realised he must have been worried. Why? Did he fear that the images would no longer speak to him? That he no longer would feel the same strong urge to finish the project? He wasn't sure. It somehow felt more complex, deeper. That perhaps he would find there was no longer any connection between his old self and his art, and the person he had become.

But it felt exactly the same. The same excitement and over-whelming sense of urgency, as if time was of the essence.

He took his hands off the keyboard and leaned back on his chair, staring intently at the image. He had to find a way of finishing this project. He had no choice. This was quite simply the project of his life.

WHEN OTTO OPENED THE door they stood face to face for a moment, both a little startled by the sight of the other. Elias held out the bottle of champagne he had bought for Otto from France.

'Come in, come in,' Otto said, and accepted the gift.

In the kitchen Otto had set the table as usual — for two. Elisabeth was clearly not coming.

'A drink?'

Elias accepted a beer, and Otto poured himself a glass of rosé.

'Clearly this holiday has been good for you,' he said, looking at Elias.

'You, too!' Elias laughed.

'Yes, it's been a really nice couple of weeks.' Otto placed a bowl of salad on the table, and another with new potatoes sprinkled with fresh dill. 'And I'm not just referring to the weather!' He opened the oven and pulled out a plate of fried Baltic herring. He sprinkled a little chopped dill on them too and placed them on the table.

'Cheers, then, Elias, and welcome back!'

They raised their glasses in a toast, and began to eat.

'I'VE BEEN SPENDING THE evenings in the courtyard,' Otto said when they had finished eating. 'Shall we take our drinks down there?'

Elias nodded and they stood up from the table. Otto gave Elias the opened bottle of wine and told him to help himself to beer from the fridge. He took his own wine glass and he picked up a plastic bag by the door.

'It's been like this every evening since Midsummer,' Otto said as they sat down. 'Quite magical. A time outside of time, somehow. Mornings that become days that turn into evenings and then nights without you even noticing, one seamlessly seguing into the other. I feel so very privileged to be able to absorb it all. No duties, nothing to attend to. I can allow myself to sink into this extraordinary time and completely let go of all thoughts of tomorrow. And yesterday, for that matter. I can be right here, right now, and this is all there is.'

He looked at Elias with a thoughtful expression.

'Do you know, Elias, I have never ever in my life experienced anything like this. Everything feels new to me. It's astonishing. I'm walking through a new landscape, where every turn offers something new. New perfumes, new sights.'

He paused.

'And I believe I know what it is. Quite simply, I am happy.'

'Weird. You've found the words for exactly what I had in mind to say,' he said.

Otto held out his glass and they toasted again.

'I can tell you've had a good time too,' Otto said.

Elias smiled again.

'When I left I had no idea what to expect. How things would evolve. I'd only met Paul a couple of times here in Stockholm. Not much to go on. But for the first time in my life I knew I didn't want to let it go. I was prepared to take the risk of being disappointed. Or hurt, or betrayed. Any risk, really. I knew it would be worth it.'

'But it was no disappointment, that's absolutely clear to see.'

Elias blushed.

'No. It was . . . well, like you said, I think I know what it is. I am happy.'

'Let us hold on to this moment, you and I. Remember how we feel right this moment. Let's promise each other that we will never forget.'

He held out his hand across the table, and Elias took it in his.

'Were you thinking Elisabeth would be joining us tonight? Were you hoping to get to see her?'

'Oh, well, I'm not sure. I did wonder if she would be coming.'

'Well, I thought we should have this evening just for the two of us. Get to talk a little.'

Elias nodded.

'I suppose you're wondering if I have read her manuscript.'

'And have you?'

Otto bent down and picked up the plastic bag, placing it between them on the table.

'I have. It's a film script. But you already knew that, didn't you? But before I go there, I need to tell you a bit about Elisabeth. It's mostly things I have found on the internet, or things I have deduced from the little she has told me herself. And from what I have read.'

He gestured towards the plastic bag.

'Since she gave this to you, I believe she wants us both to understand her story. Even if she can't tell it to us herself.'

'Okay.'

'Elisabeth used to be Elisabeth Abelin. You recognise the name?'

Elias shook his head.

'Nor did I. But I don't know much about film, and even less about French film. But I've come to understand that Elisabeth is quite a well-known actress, with many films under her belt, all directed by her then husband, David Abelin. They met when Elisabeth was at the Royal Dramatic Theatre's acting school here in Stockholm. She was only about twenty, I think. He was considerably older. I've not seen any of their films, but I thought perhaps you and I could rent some or perhaps you could help me download them. I know nothing about such things, as you know.

'Anyway, after they made seven successful films together, David Abelin began to look for another, younger actress. The old story, but in this case very public and devastating for Elisabeth, because they shared their private lives as well as their professional ones. And this,' Otto indicated the bag on the table, 'this is a script Elisabeth wrote based on diaries she kept during the last, difficult years. It's the story of the disintegration of their marriage. It's a difficult read — at least it was for me. It's so terribly honest; it seems to hold back nothing. She certainly doesn't spare herself. In fact, she doesn't seem to accuse anybody or apportion blame. She doesn't even mention his adultery. To me it seems she's writing in an attempt to understand what's happening when her marriage unravels against her will. How she comes to lose her foothold and her perspective. She's opening up her innermost self. It's truly difficult to read.'

Otto rubbed his hand over his chin.

'I can't give an opinion on the quality. Partly because I have no experience of reading scripts, and partly because I am biased, I suppose.'

Elias noticed that Otto smiled a little, as if embarrassed, but he said nothing.

'I don't think it's bad; I'm sure it could have made a good film. And I think Elisabeth believed they would make the film together, she and David. I think she really did. Like a swansong. One last joint project and a public ending to a public relationship. So she gave him the script to read.'

Otto poured himself more wine, took a mouthful and swallowed hard. It looked like he was struggling to collect himself. When he continued, his voice sounded close to breaking.

'It was made into a film. *Broken Wings* it's called. Or *Ailes Brisées.* But it's not Elisabeth's film. Not the script she wrote. David "revised" it and from all accounts made a total hash of it. He made the role of the young new wife the female lead and the ageing actress was cast as the bitter ex-wife. The point of view was no longer the double one, as in Elisabeth's script, but entirely the perspective of the male lead. It became the story of his journey out of a stagnant marriage. The older wife became an obstacle in the way of his path to a wonderful new relationship, a part virtually without a voice. Elisabeth's painfully honest script was hijacked and vandalised. By her husband.'

Elias sat absolutely still, elbows on the table, his chin in his hands.

'Oh my God. She must have been devastated,' he said.

'Clearly. Their relationship was obviously so close, so very intimate. It seems like they lived every aspect of their lives together, collaborated on everything. He was the director and she was usually the leading lady, but you get the impression that they inspired each other and cooperated on virtually everything. I suppose that's how it ought to be with the one you love, you want to give everything. You don't feel the need to hold anything back because you are one. You share everything. Give each other all that you have to give.'

Otto seemed to be lost in thought.

'So then what happened?' said Elias impatiently.

'Well, I can't be certain exactly what happened. But this was the first script Elisabeth had written on her own. She had not been given a part in any of her husband's films for several years. I think initially she saw the scriptwriting as an extension of the diaries she was keeping, but gradually she began to hope it might lead her onto a new career path. That she would be able to write for film. Perhaps even direct. But she wasn't sure if her script was good enough so she gave it to him to read.'

'And he stole it.' Elias was shaking his head in disbelief.

'I think you can say he stole not just her creation, but also the future she was hoping for. It would be nice to think she could have taken a measure of comfort from the fact that the film was so widely panned. But I suspect she saw it as proof of how bad her script had been.'

'Do you suppose she saw the film?'

'No idea. It's not clear what happened. I suspect she took off but I don't know where she went. My guess is that she was in such a bad state she needed care. In France, where she had lived for so long, or here in Sweden — I don't know. All we know is that she appeared here this winter.'

Elias rubbed his arms and shivered.

'It's getting a little chilly,' said Otto. 'Shall we go inside? Do you want to hear more about the script itself or shall we call it a day?'

'I think it will have to wait. I need to think.'

'Another day, then. Whenever you feel like it. Just let me know.'

They stood up and picked up their glasses. The gravel crunched underfoot as they crossed the courtyard, followed by a soft thud as the door closed behind them.

33

IT WAS A MOST peculiar process. She wrote through the pale nights. The time of the blackbird. She often heard it singing as she started, and heard it again when she finished. The nights expanded and sometimes felt endless, yet they were shorter than ever.

The days offered peaceful everyday life. A kind of warmth and comfort she had never before experienced. Most mornings they went to the outdoor pools at Eriksdalsbadet and swam. They had discovered that they shared an inherent, natural pace. They swam length after length, often almost alone in the pool, and every morning felt like a new beginning, a pleasure that never ceased to surprise her. Afterwards, they often went to the little café across Ringvägen and had coffee and a freshly baked Danish pastry. Elisabeth felt a faint echo of breakfasts in Paris. But it was a distant, remote memory, and thinking about it no longer hurt.

Some days they took the ferry to Djurgården and walked for hours. Lay in the grass and looked up into the eternal blueness above them. Even when she lay with her eyes closed, she could feel Otto's eyes on her. And when she opened her eyes she would find him lying on his side, his head resting in his hand and with his amber eyes on her. Still filled with the original astonished delight as if he couldn't quite fathom how it had happened. Or even what had happened.

He is happy because he loves, she thought. And the more she thought about it, the more obvious it became that this was the essence of happiness. To love was the miracle. And it struck her that she loved him. Not because he loved her, but for his boundless gratitude for his love. Perhaps it was not him she loved, exactly, but his capacity for this unselfish love. His genuine astonishment over the fact that he had been granted the gift of experiencing this.

She never tired of looking into his eyes, exploring their expression. Perhaps it was the fact that they were the same colour as hers. It was like looking into her own eyes, and finding them filled with this pure love. The expression of innocent joy never ceased to fascinate her. Indeed, it filled her with something that she reluctantly, and with a little trepidation, had to acknowledge as a measure of happiness.

They often had dinner at Otto's, and at least once a week Elias joined them. Time drifted, days of summer that subtly deepened in colour and saturation. The chestnuts in the churchyard offered leafy deep-green shade and the roses along the wall began to bloom. A warm kind of stillness had embraced the entire city, and it felt almost sensual.

———

IT WAS TUESDAY MORNING and Elisabeth was still in bed. Her eyes rested on the drawing on the opposite wall. Now that she felt she knew the bird better, it had gained a personality. More often than not she talked to it. Described how her manuscript was evolving. Asked for advice when she felt unsure about something.

The Woman in Green was now just a hazy shadow, but she

was still there. Like a fourth aspect to her existence. There were the mornings and the days with Otto. Evenings with him and sometimes also Elias. And then the solitary nights of writing. But there were cracks in this comfortable existence; cracks through which she could still discern the darkness. And she could feel the temptation to return. Back to the peace of having no needs, no expectations, no hope. The absolute emptiness in which there could be no disappointments and where there was no time. And there, in the darkness, she resided eternally: the Woman in Green.

'I am here, Elisabeth. Here, behind you, all the time. Turn away from the light and you will always be able to see me. Hear me.'

Elisabeth closed her eyes, but she could still feel the ray of sunshine that had found its way through the gap in the curtains and lay as a warm reminder across her face. A reminder of the day outside. Of life.

She folded the sheet down and sat up.

———

ELIAS WAS ALREADY THERE when she entered the kitchen. Otto was busy finishing cooking and music played in the background.

I must remember this, she thought as she stood in the doorway. The faint light from the chandelier that is superfluous on a summer evening, yet so perfect. The smell of food mixing with the fragrances of the early evening air. The obvious connection and bond between these two people. I will store it all and never let it go.

'Come in, Elisabeth. Help yourself to some wine and have a seat by the window. Dinner's almost ready. Not much of a dinner today, I am afraid. Just a plate of warm vegetables and a leg of smoked lamb, a lamb-fiddle.'

And with that he presented a large plate with green beans, peas, young carrots and new potatoes, sprinkled with herbs and a little melted butter. A smoked leg of lamb on its own board and small pots with grated horseradish and mustard. Elisabeth sipped the cool rosé. She could not contain an urge to smile.

Otto started to carve the meat. Elisabeth watched him, impressed by his skill.

'I love watching you busy yourself with food. I love how everything you create is made with such love and care.'

He looked surprised.

'Really?' He smiled, a little flustered. 'I do enjoy it, I really do. Always have. None of the women in my life have been particularly interested in cooking. My mother had no time for housekeeping so from quite a young age I started to surprise her by having dinner ready when she came home from work. She was always very appreciative of my efforts. Then, when I met Eva, I just sort of continued. I don't think we even discussed it — I just knew she wasn't the domestic type. I must admit, though, that cooking for you two has been much more satisfying.'

He served them both some thin slices of meat, and they helped themselves to vegetables.

'There's something I'd like to ask you two,' Otto said after a few mouthfuls. 'The thing is, I have a friend who has a country house on a small island in the Stockholm archipelago. Every year in August he offers me the use of it for a week or two. I was wondering if you'd both like to come with me this year. It's not far — just a short boat trip from Saltsjöbaden. You can come and go as you like — join me for the whole time, a few days, or even just over the day. There's plenty of room for us all. He's offered me the second and third week of August. I have a slight preference for the third week, because by then all the summer people will have gone back home. It's so pleasant and peaceful at that time of year. Still summery, although the nights are black. Often with starry skies.'

'Sounds lovely,' Elisabeth said. 'But I'm not sure . . .'

Otto's expectant smile faded.

'How about you, Elias? What do you say?'

Elias also seemed to hesitate.

'Only if it suits,' Otto said quickly. 'Of course I understand if you have other plans.'

'It's not that. But the thing is . . .' He looked a little uncomfortable.

'Well, Paul will be here in August. We've not sorted out exactly when; it depends on his work.'

'But that would be perfect! You might want to show him a bit of our archipelago? He is most welcome to join us, of course.'

Elias smiled.

'Thank you. I'll talk to Paul and let you know.'

'Wonderful. Shall we go downstairs to the courtyard?'

OTTO AND ELISABETH STAYED on after Elias had gone back inside. Otto pulled her close.

'Cold? Shall we go inside?'

She shook her head.

'Soon. But not yet.'

She looked at him.

'I've decided to give it a try. With Elias's images.'

Otto looked surprised.

'That's wonderful, Elisabeth! I'm sure you will do an excellent job.'

'I'm not. I'm not sure about anything — the form or the content. But I can't stop thinking about it, so I might as well give it a try. It's like it's something I just have to do. Get it out of my system. Those damned images haunt me day and night. I don't seem to be able to get them out of my head. But it's not a book I see.'

'No?'

'No. It's a film. I should have known from the very beginning. Each image moved for me. I could see where it was coming from and where it was going.'

Otto lifted Elisabeth's hand and kissed it.

'If that's what you feel, well, you just have to give it a go, don't you?'

Elisabeth put her hand on his cheek.

'You're a wise man, Otto,' she said with a smile. 'And I will.

But it won't be my film. It will be Elias's. Because it was only when I saw his images that I realised something I have never understood before. I could see the story that I have been wanting to tell all along. It was nothing like what I tried to write before. It felt surreal, because it was Elias telling my story in his images. As if he understood it better than I did. So it will be his film, not mine. An animated film with his images, and my words. *If* it becomes a film. I may have misinterpreted the whole thing, and he may not be interested. It's entirely up to him. But I will try to write this script, as a gift. In a way my gift to myself, as much as a gift to Elias.'

Otto put his arm around her shoulders again, so that they shared the warmth of their bodies. But she gently pulled away and turned to face him.

'Otto, I'd like you to promise me something.'

He started and looked at her and she thought he blanched — fright, or fear, or sadness, she didn't know. She took his hands in hers.

'I just want you to promise me you'll help Elias. Promise me you'll help him manage my words. Fill in and improve as required. Explain. Help him make this film. If that turns out to be what he wants to do.'

It was absolutely silent. Otto pulled her close and held her hard. She felt his breath against her hair.

'All that you want me to do, you can do yourself, Elisabeth. And better than I ever could. I know nothing about things like this.'

She didn't respond.

He gently lifted her chin so he could see her face. 'Why do you want me to promise this?' he asked.

'Because I think it's you that he will need, Otto.'

He kept looking at her and it was a long time before he answered.

'I promise. But I will need you, Elisabeth.'

They sat in silence.

'I think the blackbird has finished singing for this year,' he said finally. 'But we have heard it and we'll remember it, won't we?'

'We have.'

'It's getting darker day by day. But this makes the stars so much brighter. Just wait until you get to Ekholmen. The sky there is spangled with stars. We can sit on the veranda with the sea in front of us, invisible in the darkness, but ever present as a scent and a sound. And the stars above us.'

Just as he stopped talking, a blackbird started singing. Not nearby, but somewhere beyond the courtyard.

'I was wrong, Elisabeth. It's singing for us. One last time.'

Even though she could not see his face, she knew he was weeping.

———————

IT WAS ALWAYS A major readjustment, returning to her own apartment. The silence felt deafening and the darkness somehow more dense. It was not in any way frightening, just so completely different. It was as though all light had been gathered upstairs and only darkness remained down here.

She sat down by the laptop and turned it on, then switched on the small lamp in the window and slowly leafed through the pile of paper next to the computer. About halfway through, she placed the pages she had looked at to one side and focused on the rest. On top was a drawing of a dark figure, half turned away, its face invisible. The impression was of an almost weightless body, its feet not quite attached to the ground beneath it. The arms were outstretched and the hands open.

Elisabeth leaned closer, scanning every detail of the image.

She has nothing, she wrote.

> *The ground is falling away and her feet are frantically feeling for a hold. She is not floating upwards but rather is completely still. But she has just lost contact with the ground, with everything. Her hands are groping for something to hold on to, but they reach into thin air. There is no up or down. No forwards. No backwards. Just this weightless, inexplicable now, with no connection to anything . . .*

She stood up and fetched the roll of tape from the kitchen drawer. Tore off a small strip and attached it to one of the cupboard doors. She stuck the paper onto the tape and pressed it firmly in place. As she sat down again she looked up at the drawing, as if trying to see something new in it from this distance. Then she nodded to herself. And smiled.

34

'COME IN,' OTTO SAID. 'So good to see you. Hungry?'

Elias nodded and smiled.

'But that's not why I am here.'

'No?'

'Well, you're not knocking on the floor any more, so I can never be sure when it suits you.'

'No, I know. But I thought that by now you knew that I am always open. This restaurant of mine never closes to my regulars.'

They walked into the kitchen.

'On the other hand, without prior booking, you'll have to accept what the house has to offer.'

Elias sat down at the table.

Otto opened a bottle of white wine, held it up with a silent question and poured two glasses. They raised them and toasted.

'Just a salad today, I am afraid. Chicken. Hope that's all right.'

'Fine, just fine. Thank you. Like I said, I didn't really come to eat.'

'At dinner time?' Otto raised his eyebrows.

'I know.' Elias laughed.

Otto started setting the table.

'How is Elisabeth?' Elias asked.

'Oh, she's fine,' Otto said with his back to Elias. 'I see her most days. We go for a swim in the mornings.'

He sat down.

'But she's not joining us tonight?'

Otto shook his head but offered no explanation.

'I've talked to Paul,' Elias said. 'He was thrilled. Everybody has heard of the Stockholm archipelago. It might even beat Provence. Anyway, we're very happy to accept your invitation. Looking forward to it hugely. You'll have to tell us what to bring.'

'Wonderful,' Otto said. 'I'll have a think and let you know. Elisabeth says she hopes to come as well. There's just something she needs to finish . . .'

'Is she working on something? That's good news, isn't it?'

Otto laid down his knife and fork and looked at Elias.

'I think she's writing your text.'

'What?'

'She is, Elias. She is writing your words.'

'But—'

'I know, she said she couldn't. Or wouldn't. But then she changed her mind, I think.'

'Wow, that's just—'

Otto silenced him.

'She's not writing a book, though.'

Elias looked bewildered.

'She's writing a film script.'

'But she already did that, and—'

'Yes, but she's writing another one. A new one. Or rather, the one she's writing now might be the one she should have written in the first place. She's writing the film that your images made her see. That's more or less how she described it.'

Elias folded his arms across his chest, took a deep breath and exhaled loudly.

'I'll be damned.'

'Yes. And it's for you, you know. She's watching your drawings move. She told me she can *see* the film. An animated film based on your drawings. She just wants to find the words that will make others see it as well. And, more than anything, the right words for you.'

'An animated film? With my images?'

Elias jumped up from his chair, walked across to the window and threw it open. He took a few deep breaths of the cool evening air. Turning back to Otto, he spread his arms wide.

'Fucking hell, Otto! Fucking hell!' He grabbed Otto's shoulders, his eyes wide with excitement.

Otto smiled.

'Sorry about the language. I am so damned . . . well, totally stunned.'

'I haven't seen any of the script yet. I have no idea what it will be like. But she said it will be very different from her other one. Even though she feels it's almost the same story, this script will be completely different because your pictures made her see things she hadn't seen before. You have told her story so that it has become comprehensible to her. It's hard to imagine a greater compliment. But it will be your film — she is quite clear about that.'

Elias paced back and forth in the kitchen, stroking his hair and shaking his head, unable to take it all in.

The sun was lower in the sky: summer was past its peak. The wall of the building facing the courtyard was illuminated by the saturated evening light, which in turn was refracted in Otto's crystal chandelier. But it was only a matter of minutes before the entire courtyard would be in shade.

'I still don't get it. Why hasn't she said anything to me?'

'I might have put my foot in it. Thinking about it now, I realise she might have wanted to tell you herself. In her own time. It would be good if you could wait for a bit and not say anything. Until we know what she wants to do.'

'Of course, of course. It's just so . . . damned exciting! I'd never even thought about a film. Never! But now I can't stop thinking about it. I just want to run downstairs and talk to her. It's not going to be easy to wait. Not now that I know.'

'But it would be good if you could try. Let her tell you in her own way, and in her own time.'

'Of course. My brain is racing. Everything is falling into place. As if this were the plan from the start. You know, sometimes when you look back you can see that . . . well, you know, that everything just fits. All of it.'

He leaned back on the chair, clasped his hands behind his head and shook his head while his unseeing gaze was directed at the open window.

'Bloody hell . . .'

Otto smiled.

'Shall we move to the living room? Have a brandy and listen to some music?'

35

SHE WAS COLD. It was a long time since she had felt cold. She had lived first in her own feverish heat, then in the warmth of the summer. But now she was cold. She stood up and closed the kitchen window. It was dark outside and she saw herself reflected in the glass. A dark silhouette, nothing more. She sat down and turned on the computer.

The writing, which had initially run more or less instinctively, had gradually subsided and now she had to search for each word. The sentences evolved slowly and she stopped herself again and again, going back over the text. Reread. And erased. With each new attempt it took longer to reformulate sentences and paragraphs. She was afraid. Afraid of what the words would express. But most of all she was afraid of being finished.

She stood up and poured herself a glass of water. Her fingers felt stiff and she shivered as she felt the cold liquid pass down her throat. She went to the bedroom to find a jersey.

The bird was in its place on the wall. But it was strange how differently it appeared to her, day by day. The picture was the same, of course, but the effect of it had undergone a gradual change. She walked closer. What had touched her initially — the resigned, the broken and the dirty — now affected her very differently. All life had left the bird, the small wings had come to a complete rest. The beak was closed, as were the eyes. Yet somehow, the image no longer inspired the same feeling of despair. It was all over. It was free.

She pulled the jersey over her head and returned to the kitchen.

———————

B.   Don't be sad. You are not me. What
     happens to me is of no relevance. I am not
     you. I never was. I could never be all that
     is you.
E.   Then who am I?
B.   Oh, that I cannot tell you. That is for you
     to understand.
E.   I need you. Please, stay with me.
B.   You have never needed me. It was always
     I who needed you.

———————

SHE LOOKED UP AND realised that dawn was approaching outside. It was morning. She stood up stiffly and stretched. She no longer felt cold at all. The last few hours had slipped away in no time. It was finished.

She plugged the memory stick into the computer. With a click of the mouse she dragged the document across and into the drive. Just a few seconds it took. Strange how so many hours of work had become a weightless document that could fly anywhere in an instant. She unplugged the memory stick, placed it on the table beside the computer and left the kitchen.

The books sat where she had left them: in piles along one wall of the living room. But there was a kind of order to them and she quickly found what she was looking for. A small, slim volume that she carried with her back to the kitchen.

She sat down on the chair close to the window and began to read.

It didn't take long: the entire book was no longer than a short story. Yet she had always felt that it contained virtually everything human. Hope and despair. Good and evil. Gogol's *The Overcoat*.

But now something had happened to this, too.

She took a pen from the mug on the table and opened the book at the fly-leaf. She hesitated for a moment with the pen above the page. Then she began to write.

Dearest Otto
I know your bookcases are full. But this is a very slim little book. You may already have it. If so, you may find a new home for it.

For a long time I considered this book one of my absolute favourites. I thought this slight volume contained everything human. But when I read it now, I realise that I no longer see the same things in the text. Yet the text has not changed, of course. So it must be me. I must have changed. This story contains no hope; it contains only darkness. I can see that now.

Because you have changed me, Otto. You are something very rare: a good man. And you have given me hope.

I am not sure how to handle this, but that is what has happened.

I want you to know this.

Elisabeth

She put the book to one side and picked up another one that sat on the table. It was the one she had given to Elias. *Letters to a Young Poet*. She flicked through it. Stopped to read a passage here and there. Halfway through, she stretched out her hand for the pen again. As she was writing, she flicked back and forth between the fly-leaf and the page that she was holding open. When she was finished, she read out to herself what she had written:

Dear Elias

So, here is the book, back to you finally. I want you to keep it, even if you don't need to read it again. It is already in your head, I know.

The film script that I once wrote was so very dark. Now, I am glad it was never made into a film. When I began to write your story, I expected it to have a similar tone. But to my astonishment I discovered that it grew lighter as I was writing. Your bird has no broken wings. It has stamina and courage. And it has hope. I hope you can see this, too. Both in your images, and in my script.

And I hope it will be clear for all to see in the film.

Finally, Elias, a quote from 'our' book:

'To love is also good: for love is difficult. Fondness between human beings: that is perhaps the most difficult task that is set us, the ultimate thing, the final trial and test, the work for which all other work is only preparation.'

With love
Elisabeth

SHE HAD CLEARED THE kitchen table completely and placed *The Overcoat* to one side. On top of it sat her black diary. On the other side of the table, on top of the book she had once given Elias, she had placed the two memory sticks: the one Elias had given her with his images on it, and the one she had bought and which now contained the new film script.

OTTO OPENED THE DOOR with a surprised smile.

'Elisabeth!' he said. 'Come in.'

He took her hand, pulled her inside and closed the door. Then he held her in his arms for a moment before examining her face with a concerned expression.

'You haven't slept, have you?'

She shook her head.

'No. I wanted to finish it.'

'And did you?'

She nodded.

'Coffee?'

'Thank you,' she smiled.

'Music?'

She sat back and closed her eyes. She knew she must be tired, but that was not how she felt. She was strangely alert. But also exposed. Vulnerable. As if everything around her touched her in a way she had never experienced before. The very room. The scents. The music. It was as though her body and its senses had given up all resistance and now absorbed everything.

She opened her eyes when she heard Otto returning. He carried a small tray with cups and a basket of bread. The coffee aroma blended with the room's other smells to form a whole, too complex to analyse but infinitely satisfying.

Suddenly she was overwhelmed by a sense of sadness. Unbidden, she found her eyes fill with tears.

She waved her hand dismissively and tried to smile.

'Ignore me, Otto. I'm just tired.'

He sat down close to her and put his arm around her shoulders. She leaned into him and he stroked her hair.

'I am so looking forward to coming to your island, Otto. I just wanted you to know that.'

He looked at her and smiled.

'You have just made me so very happy, Elisabeth.'

SHE LAY FULLY CLOTHED on her bed, with her hands clasped on her chest. She had closed the curtains but it made little difference in the middle of the day. It was impossible to shut out the daylight. She could see no trace of the Woman in Green, but she could hear her.

'What is it that you are hoping for, Elisabeth? Do you not know that hope and disappointment belong together?'

'I'm not hoping,' Elisabeth said. 'So the thought of disappointment doesn't scare me. I am not afraid.'

'We are all afraid, you must know that. If we live, we have hope. And when we have hope, we have something to lose.'

'You're right. Fear is tied to hope. If there is no hope, then there is nothing to fear. I have no hope. And I am not afraid.'

'But can you really live without hope, Elisabeth? Hope steals upon you the moment you return to life. The most innocent situations germinate it.'

The room was completely silent.

'They say hope is the last thing to leave us. The only place you can fend off hope is here. And only if you give up all else.'

'I just want to—'

'Yes, Elisabeth, tell me what it is you want.'

'I just want to be there. I want to feel the warmth.'

'But that is exactly what is impossible, Elisabeth. Because that is hope.'

36

IT WAS A VERY small island — more of an islet. Grey granite and some low pines, twisted and gnarled by the wind, and bushes. From the landing where they had left the boat no buildings were visible.

'The entire island is ours,' Otto said, opening his arms wide to embrace it all. Here, we do exactly as we like.'

He picked up his luggage, and Elias and Paul followed, carrying the big chilly bin between them.

We could be a family on holiday, Elisabeth thought as she watched them. Dad in the lead, then the boys. And the mother. She smiled as she picked up her bag and some of the grocery bags and followed.

Elisabeth wasn't sure what she had expected. But when she saw the house, or rather the houses, she was stunned. It seemed to have the same effect on Elias and Paul, who had both stopped in their tracks, staring. It was not that it was grand. Perhaps not even beautiful. But it was just . . . absolutely perfect. The low grey wooden buildings looked as if they had always been there, an integral part of the island itself. There was a wide deck all along the front of the main building. There were two smaller buildings, and one of them also had a deck, making it look like a younger relative of the main building.

'I suggest you two take that house,' Otto said to Elias and Paul, and pointed to the smaller building. 'It's completely self-contained, with its own bathroom and a small kitchen. But you're welcome to come to the main house any time you wish, of course. I just thought you'd appreciate a bit of privacy.'

Elias and Paul gleefully grabbed their bags and wandered off in the direction of the small house.

Otto looked up at the sky.

'You can't see them, Elisabeth, but they're there, I assure you.'

He took her hand and kissed it.

'I'll show you tonight.'

———

AFTER SETTLING IN, they spent the day pottering about, mostly down by the water. Paul and Elias served lunch on the veranda and Elisabeth organised coffee on the rocks. They swam in the surprisingly tepid water and delighted in the gentle late-summer sun.

Otto had volunteered to do all the cooking, but it transpired that he had a keen assistant in Paul. The two of them were busy preparing the night's first dinner in the main kitchen. Elisabeth and Elias were setting the table on the deck.

'I'm so glad you decided to come,' Elias said. 'It wouldn't have been the same without you.'

'Or without you,' she said and smiled. 'I always wanted to come. I just had something I needed to do, and I wasn't sure it would be finished in time.'

Elias was folding the napkins, and Elisabeth noticed he was taking an inordinate amount of care with the coarse linen. She walked around the table to stand behind him, and put her arms around him.

'Thank you,' she said to his back.

He returned her embrace, and then looked at her, surprised.

'What for?'

'Oh . . . everything. I want to thank you for many things, but most of all for calling through my letterbox.'

Elias raised his eyebrows and blushed a little.

'I felt totally stupid afterwards,' he said.

Elisabeth shook her head.

'It wasn't stupid in the least. It was kind and considerate. And it changed everything.'

Otto called from the kitchen.

'The kitchen staff need some drinks!'

'Won't be a minute!' Elisabeth called back, and went inside.

THE WEEK PASSED QUICKLY. The days were dreamlike, an existence beyond time and place. It rained one night, but they woke up to heavy dew and sunshine every morning.

They spent much of the time down on the smooth rocks by the sea.

Elisabeth came walking down the path carrying the afternoon coffee in a basket. In front of her was the sea, completely calm, glittering in the sunshine. The soil felt warm under her bare feet. It was as if summer was making one last effort for them. At the far end of the landing, Elias and Paul sat side by side, silhouetted against the saturated afternoon sky. Elisabeth thought about Elias back home, in front of the mirror that time.

I'm afraid, she thought. I'm afraid for him. Afraid that he will be hurt.

She heard Otto's steps behind her.

'Lost in thought?' he said. 'Here, let me take that basket.'

'It's just so beautiful,' she said, and handed him the basket. 'But it will end, won't it?'

247

'Yes, it will. But something else will come along in its stead. And it will be born out of this.'

He put his free arm around her shoulders and they carried on down the path.

———————

THEY HAD FINISHED DINNER and were sitting in the soft darkness on the veranda. Paul had poured them each a glass of calvados, and lit the citronella candles to repel the mosquitos.

'Thank you for including me, Otto,' he said, raising his glass. 'I'll never forget this week.'

He smiled broadly and Elisabeth was struck once more by how handsome he was. The white teeth against the olive skin, the dark hair curling at the nape of his neck. The beautiful hands. He was wearing a white shirt, unbuttoned and with the sleeves rolled up.

They reached across the table and clinked their glasses.

'This is how we should always live.' Paul made a sweeping gesture with his hand to take in all that lay beyond their small circle of light. 'So you could catch up with yourself.'

'Perhaps. But I'm not sure what it would be like to sit here through the long dark winter.'

'Oh, with the right company I think it would be all right,' Paul said, with his hand on Elias's arm.

'I'm sure you are right. Place is unimportant if you have the right company.'

Elias leant towards Elisabeth, his hands flat on the table in front of him. He looked straight at her.

'There's something I have to ask,' he said. 'I just can't hold back any longer.'

Elisabeth turned to catch his gaze and she looked pale, her face a white oval with large dark eyes.

'Otto tells me you have written a manuscript. A new script.'

Elisabeth freed herself from Otto's arm and bent forward to take Elias's hands in hers.

'Yes, that's right,' she said. 'I have written a manuscript. A film script. But I'm not sure you'll like it. You see, as I was writing, my vision of what I was doing changed.'

Elias kept his eyes on her, and he held on to her hands.

'I knew that I had somehow inspired those first few drawings you did. But I couldn't understand why. You hadn't even met me.'

Elias said nothing.

'When you first let me see the images, I did see myself in that little bird. I didn't mind you seeing me as a bird. Quite the opposite, in fact. As you know, I had called my own manuscript *Broken Wings*. There's something about birds . . .'

She paused and looked at Elias for some response. Nothing was forthcoming so she continued.

'They're so fragile, so terribly exposed. You can break the neck of a blackbird with your fingers. Yet it can rise high above us. Fly far beyond our reach.'

A lengthy silence followed and the soft sound of the sea surrounded them.

'So, yes, Elias. There is a manuscript waiting for you back home. It's yours to do what you like with. I'm not sure that it's worthy of your images, but it's the best I can do.'

Elias lifted her hands and kissed them.

'Thank you,' he whispered. 'Thank you, Elisabeth.'

Elisabeth glanced across at Paul. He sat leaning back, his right hand clasping and unclasping the arm of his chair. His unseeing eyes were set on a point somewhere behind her head.

'I apologise, Paul. Here we are chatting away in Swedish.'

His eyes met hers. He pursed his lips in what seemed like a strange little smile. It lasted only a few seconds, and she realised she might have misinterpreted it completely. But the expression on his face had seemed slightly mocking. Cold. And his hand jiggling, as if he were holding back irritation. Elias seemed completely oblivious.

There was a brief lull in the conversation. Suddenly Paul pushed back his chair and stood up. Without a word he left the table, whistling as he went. Elisabeth thought he walked with an exaggerated swagger, somehow again giving a taunting impression. After a moment he returned holding a bottle of champagne and the stems of four glasses.

'There are certain moments when nothing other than champagne will do. I consider this such a moment. I am a Frenchman, after all. We don't need much excuse to drink champagne.' He smiled and his dark eyes twinkled in the light from the candles as he opened the bottle and poured.

Elias walked around the table towards Elisabeth. She stood close to him and ran her palm softly over his cheek, then reached up to give him a kiss. He put his arms around her and they stood silently in a tight hug. A strange solemnity settled over them.

The moment was interrupted by Paul clearing his throat loudly.

'Well, cheers, and good luck for the film. And everything else,' he added, and they all raised their glasses and drank.

Otto pulled Elisabeth close.

'This is only the beginning, Elisabeth. Only the beginning.'

She looked at him, but said nothing, still unnerved by what she thought she had seen in Paul. And when Paul put his arm around Elias's shoulders, it wasn't Elias whom he looked at, but Elisabeth. She couldn't interpret his expression this time either. But it made her feel uncomfortable.

She shuddered and pressed herself closer to Otto.

———

ELIAS SUGGESTED HE AND Paul should do the dishes. He pulled Paul to his feet and the two of them disappeared inside the house.

'There is such a strange silence here,' Otto said to Elisabeth. 'On the one hand it seems completely silent. But the silence is also full of small, unidentifiable sounds. But I can't hear them because my hearing is sort of tuned to another frequency. And then after I have been here a few days it changes, and I begin to distinguish more and more individual sounds. You'll see.'

Elisabeth sat close, resting her head on his chest, and he had his arm around her.

'I can hear your heartbeat,' she said.

'That's good!' He smiled.

'When I was alone in my apartment day after day, I began to notice that our building has its own sound. A kind of heartbeat too — a pulse. You can feel it if you put your hands against the wall. Especially at night.'

When the boys returned from the kitchen they said goodnight and Otto asked them to turn off the lights in the kitchen and close the sliding door before they wandered over to their own house.

Elisabeth watched them walking through the grass, disappearing as the light from the veranda no longer reached them. She felt a stab of inexplicable sadness at the sight.

Otto blew out the candles. Instantly, darkness seemed to flood the veranda.

'See? It's no longer completely dark, is it?' Otto said quietly. 'The more lights you turn off, the better you can see. And the sounds are clearer, aren't they?'

Elisabeth nodded against his chest.

'Shall we walk down and sit on the rocks by the landing for a little while before we go to bed?' Otto asked.

They made their way down to the water with the small pool of light from Otto's torch flickering ahead of them across the path.

'Come and sit here,' Otto said, and guided her to a smooth hollow space in the granite. They could hear the waves lapping against the rocks. Otto switched off the torch and for a moment all was black again.

'Lie down, Elisabeth,' he said. He stretched out alongside her and took her hand. 'Now, let's just wait a little. Close our eyes for a moment. Let our eyes adjust.' He turned his face and kissed her.

'Look,' he whispered.

Elisabeth opened her eyes.

Above them the black August sky was a sea of stars. Not individual stars, as she had always seen them before. No, here the entire sky was covered in them. Layer upon layer of stars of varying intensity, like a wide sparkling band across the sky. It was alive, scattering ever new stars in all directions.

Elisabeth turned abruptly and pressed herself against Otto. He held her tight against his body.

'I am scared, Otto,' she murmured.

'Scared?'

She said something into his chest, but he couldn't catch the words.

'But there's nothing to be scared of here, Elisabeth.'

She pressed her hand against his chest and looked up at him.

'Oh, yes there is, Otto,' she said. 'It's frightening to be happy.'

He stroked her hair and they stayed like that for a long time, pressed closely together.

———

IT WAS STILL DARK when Elisabeth opened her eyes. She felt the warmth of Otto's body nearby. He was asleep on his stomach, his head turned to her. His cheek covered in familiar silvery stubble. His arm was outstretched, his hand resting on her stomach. She closed her eyes again and listened to his soft breathing.

'Come.'

It was just the faintest sound. Not even a sound, really. It was a chill inside her and it consumed her completely. The comfortable world where Otto was sleeping fell away. She could no longer feel the warmth, sense his smell or hear his breath.

He didn't stir when she gently moved his arm, nor when she folded down the sheet and slid out of bed. She took the bathrobe that lay ready for the morning swim and soundlessly left the bedroom. The sky was a pale turquoise along the horizon to the east, but above her it was still night. She silently opened the door and stepped out onto the veranda. The wood was cold and damp under her feet. She closed the door behind her, crossed the veranda and carried on down the steps. Her eyes had adjusted to the darkness and she could follow the path without difficulty.

Once down by the water she let the bathrobe fall to her feet. She stood still for a moment, her gaze on the sky. She could only just distinguish the stars now and they appeared to be fading before her eyes. Pulling away from her . . .

She walked out onto the landing. The surface of the water was impenetrable, black, and the only sound she could hear was the lapping of the small waves against the poles below.

Let Me Sing You Gentle Songs

One bleak March evening Veronika, a young writer, arrives in a small village in pursuit of stillness and solitude.

Her arrival is silently observed by Astrid, her elderly, reclusive neighbour, who in the safety of her home guards dark family secrets and personal tragedy.

As the icy winter gives way to spring, the two women are drawn together, embarking on a tender and unusual friendship. What happens will change the lives of both women forever.

Set against a haunting Swedish landscape, *Let Me Sing You Gentle Songs* is a lyrical and meditative novel of love and loss, and a story that will remain with readers long after the characters' secrets are revealed.

Sonata for Miriam

When Adam Anker loses his daughter Miriam, he loses his hold on life. After a year of grieving, he decides to embark on a journey of discovery. His daughter's unanswered questions merge with his own: who am I?

Adam's journey takes him to Krakow, where his life once began, and where now he tracks down some mysteries from his past. To Stockholm where his life continued. And, on an island off Sweden's rocky coast, to the woman who gave his life meaning.

Sonata for Miriam is a heartbreaking tale of a man's search for his past and the importance of talking about the most vital and the most painful things in life. But more than anything it is a novel about love.

From the Author of
Let Me Sing You Gentle Songs

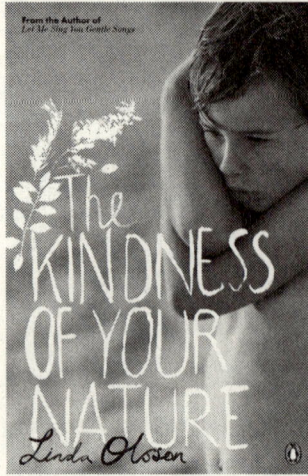

The Kindness of Your Nature

Marion Flint lives alone on the isolated west coast of New Zealand's North Island. One day she finds a small boy, Ika, lying face down on the sand of the empty, rugged beach. An unlikely friendship begins between the Swedish doctor and the silent child with webbed hands.

As Marion's involvement with Ika deepens, she is forced to revisit her own lonely childhood and the events that led her to cast herself adrift.

This beautifully written and insightful novel explores the many forms love takes — the destructive, the forbidden and, ultimately, the healing.